The Dark City and Other Stories

The Dark City and Other Stories

Surendra Mohanty

Translated from Odia by
Sambit Panigrahi

BLACK EAGLE BOOKS
Dublin, USA | Bhubaneswar, India

Black Eagle Books
USA address:
7464 Wisdom Lane
Dublin, OH 43016

India address:
E/312, Trident Galaxy, Kalinga Nagar,
Bhubaneswar-751003, Odisha, India

E-mail: info@blackeaglebooks.org
Website: www.blackeaglebooks.org

First International Edition Published by
Black Eagle Books, 2023

THE DARK CITY AND OTHER STORIES
by **Surendra Mohanty**

Translated from Odia by **Sambit Panigrahi**

Original Copyright © Surendra Mohanty
Translation Copyright © Sambit Panigrahi

Cover & Interior Design: Ezy's Publication

ISBN- 978-1-64560-459-4 (Paperback)
Library of Congress Control Number: 2023947758

Printed in the United States of America

CONTENT

Translator's Note   07

The Dark City   11
The Gulmohur   22
The Dancing Ghost   28
The Last Redemption   40
The Imprisoned Father   57
The Cursed Courtesan   66
The Smiling Krishna   78
The Yadavas   89
The Last Dinosaur   109
A Spring Night of Grief   122
The Floating Moon and the Cold Bread   134
The False Capital   143
The Wandering Gypsy   162
The Last Remnant of Flood   177

Translator's Note

Surendra Mohanty, a celebrated Odia writer and seasoned politician, was born on 21 June 1922 and he passed away in 21 December 1990. A writer of exceptional creative sensibility, Mohanty penned down many fictional and non-fictional outputs and they have continued to remain his ground-breaking contribution to the vast repository of Odia language and literature. Mohanty possessed many literary and political credentials to his credit. He was a not only a writer of great repute, but also a politician of eminence. Mohanty was the president of Odisha Sahitya Academy from 1981 to 1987. He was also the first editor, and later chief editor for the newspaper *The Sambad*. He is a writer of short stories, novels, travelogues, criticism and biographies. He wrote around 50 books belonging to different genres. Some of his well-known novels are *Nilasaila* (*The Blue Mountain*) and *Andha Diganta* (*The Dark Horizon*). *Mahanirvana* (*The Salvation*), *Yadubansa* (The Yadu Dynasty), *Mahanagarira Ratri* (*Night in the Metropolis*), *Rajadhani* (The Capital City), *Krushnachuda* (The Gulmohur) and *Ruti O Chandra* (Bread and The Moon) etc. are some of his famous short stories.

Apart from being a litterateur, he was also a politician and a member of parliament in 1957.

Translating Surendra Mohanty is an experience in itself. It's a widely acknowledged by literary critics that in his short stories, Surendra Mohanty is perhaps at his creative best. The most interesting feature about his short stories is that they are not confined to any particular theme or area; rather, they range across a wide variety of subjects including history, mythology, his contemporary society, the individual etc. The wide spectrum of themes, areas and concerns that he encompasses in his stories provide him wide acceptability as a writer amongst the audience. Mohanty seems to have developed a particular interest in Buddhism and its history for which he has penned some of his stories like "Pita Putra" ("Father and Son") and "Mahanirvana" ("The Salvation") and in my estimation, some of Mohanty's finest stories are in fact his stories based on Buddhism and its history.

As mentioned by me, Mohanty also takes interest in mythology whose biggest testimony is his story "Srikrushnanka Sesha Hasa" (Srikrishna's Last Laugh) where he draws on certain important and interesting episode of *The Mahabharata* and presents it before the audience in the form of a short story. By writing such stories, Mohanty not only displays another specimen of his phenomenal artistry as a creative writer, but also acquaints the readers with such forgotten or less known but important episodes of the great Indian epics like *The Mahabharata*.

But apart from mythological stories, Mohanty also focuses on real life stories which have emerged from his own real life experiences that range across different eras and generations from the pre-independent to the post-independent times. His story "Dinosar-ra Atma" ("The Soul of the Dinosaur") is a story that is based on the lost glory and grandeur of royalty and kingship in the post-independent era where a previous king finds himself like a dinosaur—a rare specimen of an extinct species.

Some of Mohanty's stories are also intensely political in nature where he covertly expresses his political views through his characters. One such story is "Ruti O Chandra" ("Bread and Moon") where Mohanty provides a criticism of Marxism by exposing its indifference to delicate human feelings and sentiments and its over-indulgence in economic indicators as the only determinants of human lives and human values.

But one cannot undermine the fact that one of the major features of Mohanty's narrative craft is humour—a humour that originates from his keen observations of the hypocrisy that exists in politics, in the false sophistications and intellectualism in our academia etc. Some such stories that are the best examples of Mohanty's ability to create humour in his writing are: "Rajadhani" ("The Capital"), "Vagabond" etc. where he thoroughly exposes and gleefully mocks at some of our follies and hypocrisies that we want to hide under the garbs of cultural and intellectual sophistications.

After providing a brief introduction to some of the important thematic concerns of Mohanty in his stories, I must now share with the audience some of my own experiences of translating Mohanty from Odia to English. It is famously said by eminent American poet Robert Frost that "Poetry is what is lost in translation"—a statement that is a clear indicator of how much difficult it is for the translator to carry the whole essence of the original text into the translated text. Each language is intrinsically embedded with certain cultural values and nuances specific to its own and which are perhaps untranslatable. Certain colloquial expressions, which Mohanty abundantly uses in his writing, are its best example. As a translator of Mohanty's short stories, I have tried my level best to negotiate between two languages and two cultures that are perhaps diametrically opposite to each other. It must be understood however that absolute faithfulness to the original text and the original language is an impossibility.

Mohanty, in spite of his greatness and stature as a creative writer in Odia, can at times be accused of unwarranted verbosity though I do understand that a creative writer's creative process has limitless dimensions. Translating wordy sentences and expressions may look a bit challenging, but it is also a pleasurable experience to simplify the clumsiness of certain expressions in the target language, that is English.

At the end, I would like to thank my family members including my parents and my wife and friends who stood by me all through my effort. And at last my prayer to Lord Jagannath.

Sambit Panigrahi

The Dark City

A steamer screamed fiercely in the Ganga Jetty. In the dim light of the light-post, Chaurangi's empty road looked like a mysterious and bodiless ghost from the underworld.

Chaurangi—the Mecca and Medina of business culture!

On the other side of the tram-road, clusters of refugees slept on the soil; below was the dust-ridden land of the city, and above, floated the tranquil night-sky like a dark, embroidered canopy. The roadside furnaces smouldered with fragments of burning coals.

The quiet moon walked unsteadily on the sky's stretching highway like a habitual drunkard. The dance party in a roadside western hotel was already broken and dispersed by now. From inside the hotel, a few western-dressed men were coming out in every five to ten minutes and whistling loudly at the bystanders who stood on the Chaurangi pavement. One of them asked me: "Salam Sahib! Salam! Do you want a girl?"

"Nonsense! How dare you say such a thing to me?"

11

I asked the man in a heavy and irritated voice. But it was his business. The man was a little taken aback by my crude response and then, said in a slightly apprehensive tone: "You do not have to go very far, sir; it's here, in the first bend of the Park Street."

I was surprised by the nagging confidence of the man; he stuck to me like a shade despite my clear reprimand. Heedless of his unrelenting persuasion, I kept walking ahead while trembling all across my torso in a mixed feeling of shame and anger. I wished I could shoot that man as if shooting a dog. What a fallen, an abominable creature! But I was also aware of the fact that he represented a culture that reigns here, however crude and despicable it might be. I thought if one could be a respectable leader by brooking between the nation and the individual, if one could be a reputed lawyer by doing the same between the justice system and the client, if one could be a great sage by mediating between God and man, then why should a man be condemned for pimping between the flesh of an unfortunate girl and the bestial desire of a lecher? Strange are this pimp business and its culture, I thought. You never know one day this bunch of businessmen would end up selling this nation's soul. They would earn percentage for that—what's the harm?

Another one was standing behind the pillar. Looking at me, he suddenly came in front and stood there, unmoved.

"Hey sir! Look at that advertisement board. It's not very far. It's there on the Park Street bend." He said.

I looked back. The first broker was getting inside a taxi with a western-dressed sahib. I did not pay much heed to that and kept walking ahead oblivious of what had happened so far. A horse-cab-man, while speeding up his boggy on the road, called in a loud-mouthed voice: "Come Sahib! Come! Bada Bazar! Bada Bazar! Park Street!" This was the third broker I met on the Park Street. I looked keenly at him. He went on describing the place in greater details.

I asked him this time: "Is this your income"?

He answered quite confidently: "Yes sir! Percentage and tips give me good earning."

We approached the glistening advertisement board and then, went a little ahead.

****

It was a beautiful, starlit night of March. The soil beneath emitted a heated vapour that seemed like the warm sigh of Earth. I felt asphyxiated. The roadside cotton trees were flooded with innumerable flowers; the skyscrapers looked like pigeon-nests from a distance containing thousands of families fallen asleep—husbands, wives, brothers, sisters, daughters . . . all of them.

I moved on. One street led to another sub-street which ended in a flat. Its upper storey was filled with clearly audible laughters from a few drunkards. I knew straightway that I was right there in the much-talked-about Park Street end.

A man called me from the upper storey by hitting the bolt against the door. The door opened and the lady that came out was perhaps the flat's owner. I put my head down in shame and did not really know what I was thinking. The man pushed me a bit and told: "Sahib! Tips!" I took out a five rupee note from my pocket and pushed into that man's hand. He looked immensely happy and obliged and said:

"Salam Sahib!" Then he looked at the Park Street lady and said: "Sister! Where is my due?"

I asked him: "What due?"

He said: "My percentage."

I pushed another five rupee note into that man's hand and said: "Leave now."

That man went away whistling with a tone of extreme contentment. The Park Street lady looked at me with a visible sense of bewilderment and told: "Come in sir."

My mouth was drying up. I asked while getting inside: "May I have something to drink?"

The lady answered: "Sure sir!" She then called a girl by her name: "Minu! Minu!"

A small girl of thirteen or fourteen appeared on the scene with sleepy eyes and a face that bore an expression of slight irritation. But that expression made her look even more beautiful. The Park Street lady ordered her: "Bring a glass of iced beer, Minu."

I was assured that the old lady has a gentility of taste. It made me happy. Minu left. Her sleepy and curvy wig covered her back like the sturdy arms of a lecher. A blood-red rose was dug deep into her wig. But the rose looked pale and lifeless.

I kept looking at her with transfixed eyes. The Park Street lady said: "Sahib! She is my sister. She has not been initiated yet."

She was perhaps afraid I would straightway ask for Minu's flesh. But has this flesh ever fulfilled the hunger of the body? This flesh is for the hunger of the mind. I could never have enjoyed this little girl; I could have loved her with parental affection.

Minu came back with an iced bear bottle on a tray and placed that before me.

The Park Street lady said: "Hey! Why didn't you bring cigarettes?"

Minu was going back to bring cigarettes. I interrupted and told: "I have cigarettes with me. You please sit here."

Minu sat beside me. Her eyes were getting closed. I wished she could sleep on my lap and I could tell her the enchanting stories of the prince and the princess. The prince sitting on the will-horse, the princess on his lap, the will-horse flying away with the speed of an arrow . . . And chasing them the gigantic monster from the cave. . .

Minu, while flexing her body, told: "I am going, sister." And then, she left.

Her long wig cascaded her back. But she left me with a farrago of mixed but conflicting emotions—pity, sympathy, affection, hatred, love . . .

After Minu left, I looked at the Park Street lady again. She was almost forty with a slackened skin. Her growing age was visible through the proliferating wrinkles across her face and eyes. However, she had tried her best to bear the appearance of a young lady. Her entire face was painted; she wore lipstick on her lips; her cheeks had ruse on them. But of course, all these cosmetics and extravagances could not minimize her age; rather it looked as if she has become ten years older. If she had a son, he would have been my age.

I took clear cognizance of the place again. That flat

of the Park Street bend... Two emptied beer bottles lying below the Sofa... the ashtray nearby filled with broken cigarette pieces

****

How terrible is this woman's figure? She had been a daughter, a daughter-in-law, a mother...; but today, her hunger has slaughtered them all with immense cruelty. She wants to live.

Her face reminded me of another woman.

That day I was travelling from Howra in Delhi-Punjab mail. It was a huge rush in the inter-class compartment where there was no space for even a mustard seed. I went standing from Howra to Asansol. At the corner of a long berth, a lady sat on a blanket spread on the ground. Looking at me, she said: "How long would you go standing, son? Sit here."

I sat near him shyly. But she made me comfortable by saying: "Why do you feel apprehensive, man? You are my son's age. He stays at Delhi. I am going to meet him."

Two half-circled lines came running from her nostrils to her cheek. But they were soft, shiny and graceful. If she saw me somewhere on the streets, she would have called me 'son.'

But today it is the Park Street bend; it's fifteen minutes to two o' clock. The lady sits before me with an artificial, ruse-powdered face that hides beneath its skin legion anecdotes of pain, of suffering, of misfortune.

The silence was growing unbearable for me. For a moment I thought it would have been better for me to leave this place.

I asked her: "What's your name?"

She answered: "Chandra!" Then she told in an accustomed voice: "Please come inside! How long would you sit here?"

I took out two ten-rupee notes and pushed them into Chandra's hand and told: "It's already so late in the night. I am leaving."

Chandra was perhaps thinking that she has no justified right on this unexpected money. Hence, she perhaps intended to say something when I opened the door and said:

"Give half of it to Minu."

Chandra told: "But Sir! You have not even touched her." There was a strange sense of curiosity on her varnished face."

Her question hit me like a sharp arrow. The moon-burnt night of March turned poisonous in a moment. One day Minu would be touched. Then the luxurious men of the city would eat morsels of her flesh, one after another, like hungry wild beasts with sharp, dazzling canines; they would tear apart her body with their curvy, sharpened nails. And then the day when her flesh would be completely consumed, she would be thrown away like a piece of bone into the drain. A cold shiver ran through my spine like an electric wave. There was a strange and unexplained agitation in my nerves. But I had to control myself with restraint.

****

It was twelve o' clock the next day. The same Chaurangi pavement, the same question . . .

"Do you want a girl, Sahib?"

I walked along the Park Street bend towards that flat.

The same flat! The door closed from inside! I gave it a gentle knock and it opened from inside. Minu appeared before me and told: "Come inside, Sir." I went inside and sat on the Sofa. Minu's lotus-face looked more beautiful and brighter than last night.

Then she told: "Some two people are inside. My sister would just arrive. You please be seated. Let me go and bring beer for you."

But I told: "No! I want only water."

Within some time Minu came and placed a glass of water on the table and then, was almost leaving. I told: "Minu! Please sit here."

She sat on the corner with a mixed feeling of hesitation and apprehension."

I asked: "Where are you from Minu?"

Her two eyes turned watery with these questions. Slowly two drops of tear started rolling down her cheeks.

I asked: "Why are you crying, Minu?"

She told: "My home is far distant from here, sir. We were escaping. My father was lost somewhere. My brother was hacked to death."

"My mother ended up being here . . ." Her voice was almost choking in her throat. I could understand that she had been sold in this street by her hapless mother who did so to alleviate her burden.

I felt like crying for the girl. But my tears were dried up.

I asked: Have you got some education, Minu?"

She answered: "Yes, I can read."

I took out a Rupakatha journal from my pocket and placed it in her hand and told her: "When you feel depressed, read this book."

With a girlish swiftness, she rubbed her hand a few times on the book cover on which there was pained the photo of an unknown prince. He was riding the wish-horse, on a mission to free his incarcerated princess.

Minu might be thinking the prince of her dreams would arrive. Or he might not come. The wings of the wish-horse might have broken inside the deep forest at the outskirts of the city.

I could hear Chandra's footsteps and that of her two drunken customers form the stairs. Minu left.

Those two customers also left. Chandra closed the door and sat beside me. She smelt of cheap, country-made liquor. I stepped back for the smell was nauseating.

Chandra said: "Not here today, Sir. Let's go upstairs."

I was not at all willing to go upstairs, but could not resist my inquisitive temptations and followed her all along the stairs to the playhouse at the top. The whole inner space was filled with whisky and soda bottles and cigarette strays.

Chandra sat on the sofa. Her head was reeling with the hangover of liquor.

All on a sudden my eyes were fixed on a framed photograph lying on her table. It was the photo of a handsome man. I stepped ahead to have a look.

Chandra came from the sofa like a storm and pushed the photograph inside the drawer.

I asked in a stupefied voice: "Don't worry Chandra. What is the harm in me having a look at your lover?"

Chandra started crying in a tearful voice and said: "Do you know sir who is this man? He is my son. I gave birth to him after bearing him for ten months in my womb."

He was not a bastard child, Sir. He was the son of his father. They hacked him to death that day in front of my eyes. I have seen men turn into beasts. They hacked my husband in a similar way. They spared me only for my body. I could manage to save myself with my body and come here.

Chandra hid her face on my chest and started crying like a baby. I felt like pushing her off due to the smell of liquor. But Chandra was not leaving me as she felt that crying like this might help her alleviate the pain of her tormented soul.

After some time, she lifted her head from my chest and started wiping off her tears. They were washing off the paint from her face and exposing the dark skin of her face . . . ugly and horrifying. Her skin looked like tin stripped off its tar. Two drops of tear were burning in her eyes, like two pieces of smouldering charcoals.

I took out a fifty-rupee note from my pocked and pushed into her hand and said; "I am going Chandra."

Chandra told: "No Sir! I won't leave you, those two drunkards . . ."

It was five minutes to two o' clock in the night.

I told: "No, I shall leave Chandra."

She pressed her lipstick-ridden lips against my face and told: "No, you can't leave Sir."

I felt as if someone was pressing a burning piece of coal tightly against my face. I slapped her on her face and told: "Leave me."

Chandra told in a stupefied and injured voice: "Sir.'

I told: "Not sir! If you would like to call me by some name, call me son. I would be your son's age if he was alive."

Chandra pressed her head against my face and cried: "O God!"

Outside the cruel night reverberated with that sound: "O God!"

Its echo was howling through the steamer's restless shout in Ganga Jetty.

****

The Gulmohur

The weekly newspaper *Sangram*'s office!

Sadananda was looking at the proof. The age old building looked on. The rain peeped in through the cracks of its concrete roof. Water streamed along the floor. On one side of the wall ran the blue cover of moss.

Outside, the August monsoon rain had subsided a little. In a feeling of exhaustion mixed with depression, Sadananda pushed the proof to the other side of the table. While correcting the proofs incessantly, he had turned into a depressing cynic in the last few years. His life had been a compendium of mistakes right from the beginning till the end.

Four pages still remained for the finalization of the print—sixteen columns. They had to be edited. In a feeling of exhaustion and irritation, Sadananda brought out a piece of cigarette from his pocket and lighted it.

He was simultaneously the editor and the proof reader of the weekly. One more assistant was there to take care of the external things.

For some reason, Sadananda looked back and stared at the outside environment. For the last many years, he had never looked outside with so much of keenness and passion. He could not exactly count the number of days or months or years for which he had not looked at the external world so carefully.

A Gulmohur tree stood adjacent to the window. Beautiful—No! Only the word 'beautiful' would be an incomplete description of the tree. Its reddish blooms were gorgeous, soft, sweet and soothing.

In the August sky, the dark nimbus clouds were as if touching the soil. And the lone Gulmohur tree looked like blooming in their lap like a flower.

The cigarette was finished. Sadananda threw it outside.

Sixteen columns more!

He closed the door violently. In a world made of slaves, life for him had become no more than a meaningless existence. He thought he was living the life of slavery in a world full of slaves. It had sucked the marrows form the bones of every free citizen of this world.

"Then what is the difference between a coolie form the suburb and Sadananda?" He thought. "The coolie is the slave of the mill owner and the idealistic Sadananda is the slave of his own ideology. What is the difference?" He kept muttering to himself.

Even there is a sense of fulfilment in the coolie's life. The day he gets his salary at the weekend, he drinks to the full with a sense of absolute contentment. But Sadananda did not have that luxury. A huge discontent brooded over his life right from the beginning till the end. And where was that feeling of contentment in his idealism? It was never there. Sadananda lived a life full of discontentment, of unrealized dreams.

****

The window opened on its own with a gush of wind.

The Gulmohur tree peeped at him through the window. There was a clear sense of ridicule in its look.

Too many years had passed by now. One day he had decorated Tamasa's wig with Gulmohur in his own hands. It was a long time ago, when Tamasa came to his house as a bride. That was a lazy afternoon of a torrentially raining August.

Today, Sadananda's aging hands have lost their reflexes.

Sixteen columns more!

Sadananda came back and sat near the table. But how would he have finished these sixteen columns? The treachery of Britain? The growth of feudalism in Russia? The growing capitalism of America? Or the mental illness of India? Sadananda had lost his patience in writing such stuff again and again.

One could not however write the story of this Gulmohur tree in the newspaper. This tired, red Gulmohur tree—in whose reddish luxury, this silent, cloudy August afternoon had become fickle and mischievous.

No! Gulmohur won't perhaps find a place in the editor's universe. The whole world would perhaps ridicule its description in a newspaper column.

The newspaper columns are meant only for politics where the act of living is nothing but a mere pretension, where the greed for power, domination and exploitation carries the only meaning of life. The Gulmohur has no place here.

Sadananda came back and sat near the tree.

But it seemed as if the tree had revolted against this narrow mentality. It had flown its gray banner of revolt throughout the world.

Sadananda got up from his chair like a man hypnotized by a sorcerer. Then he left the office and went outside.

The rain had stopped. Sadananda came back and stood below that Gulmohur tree. On the green grassland below were spread out the red petals of its flowers scattered by the wind.

In Sadananda's every vein, there rose the fickleness of an early youth. He wanted to get up to the tree and pluck the Gulmohur flowers as much as he liked.

But inside his own 'self,' he could not muster the courage to do so. If he plucked the flowers at this age, the world would ridicule him. Sadananda looked at all directions. There were human beings all around— innumerable, dirty, abominable bipods.

"Hey, Ramesh is coming here. He is definitely coming with some new complaints." Sadananda said to himself.

Ramesh came nearer and told: "Sadananda! The press is closed. You are roaming here. Please tell me how shall the compositors get their salary tomorrow?"

Sadananda told; "I don't know."

Ramesh aksed: "What do you mean?"

Sadananda answered: "I really don't know. You go from here Ramesh. Please don't disturb me."

Ramesh came back from there dumbfounded.

After some time, Sadanada also came back. Everywhere there were human beings. He could not muster the courage to climb up the tree and pluck the flowers.

Now it was late in the night.

In the cloud-infested sky, the pale moon of the dark night had come out.

One ray of that gloomy moonlight had fallen on the sleeping Tamasha.

But there was no sleep in Sadananda's eyes. In these eyes was dancing the reddish fickleness of the Gulmohur flowers.

Sadananda looked at Tamasha and said to himself: "This is the Tamasha on whose wig, one day I had put the cluster of these flowers."

He muttered again: "No! This is not that bride Tamasha in whose wig the mystery of that night laid hidden. That Tamasha is dead and gone."

Man dies. Man dies some day without his knowledge. The rest of his life, he lives the charmless life of a slave.

Tamasha is dead and gone. Sadananda is dead and gone.

Sadananda left his bed and stealthily went outside to that same Gulmohur tree.

The tree was gleefully swaying the canopy of its flowers over the sleeping Earth.

Sadananda came and stood below it.

He tightened his dress to climb up. But he felt as if he had become handicapped, limbless. His whole body had as if drained itself off all its youthful fickleness.

Still, Sadananda started climbing the tree, applying all his energy and strength.

Suddenly he heard a voice from behind: "Who is there?"

The constable of the night duty! He was clad with a raincoat from top to bottom. A stick in his hand! A half-burnt cigarette in his lips!

Sadananda got down from the tree.

The constable lighted his torch and focussed it on Sadananda.

"O you, Sir! So late in the night!" Said the constable.

Sadananda answered in an unprepared voice: "No! Nothing much!"

Before the constable spoke any further, Sadananda came back from that place with quickened steps.

He thought as if this Earth had died. Sadananda had died. The Gulmohur tree was only a tearful emblem of that once picturesque life.

****

The Dancing Ghost

While travelling through the main line, one encounters a small station named Madhupur on the borders of Bihar and Odisha. I had missed the 64-Up and am waiting for catching the Janata Express. I was planning to go to Banaras. If the train was on time, it would have reached at 7 in the evening. It was five more hours in the waiting. The waiting room was small. Who came to Madhupur these days? Madhupur's good days were over by now. But there was a time when a lot of rangers from Calcutta and Patna used to come to Madhupur during Durga Puja or Christmas holidays. Many of them, gotten enamoured by Madhupur's beautiful climate, its long, sprawling fields, the cool shade of its Sal forest, the blue wavy pattern of the Hazaribag mountain range at a distance etc. had built residential houses and bungalows here. A huge rangers' colony was established in Madhupur due to that. The place was crowded by the gathering of the rangers during Puja and Christmas vacations. But these days, the new generation of affluent rangers went to places like Srinagar, Darjeeling, Kalimpong, Goa, Calangute Beach, Mahabalipurum or Delhi. Madhupur was now a deserted place. Today, it was a forsaken slum.

Last year, I felt like spending my vacation in Madhupur. Instead of spending time in three-star or five-star hotels like the new generation of affluent men, I thought of spending a few quiet and peaceful days of my vacation inside a grass-infested, forsaken building. I thought I could spend some decent time in its patches of directionless shade, in its curvy roads leading to the blue, wavy patterns of the Hazaribag Mountain Range. A friend of mine had arranged for me a mossy resort here. On its dilapidated gate, you would still find an unclear inscription on a marble slab written in Bengali; "Madhukunj."

After the first day however, I felt a lot bored in Madhukunj. Its forsaken and mysterious silence was killing. By staying here, one can understand the difference between the illusory Madhupur seen through the moving train's window railings and the actual Madhupur. The difference between illusion and reality! One was a fanciful imagination and the other, a crude reality! There were two ghostly houses nearby and adjacent to them was an old house inhabited by a retired judge. The old gentle man lived there alone. With him there was a cook and a dog. Two houses away from his house, lived an ex landlord in a huge mansion. He also seldom came out of his mansion. Hotel 'Parvati' was the only place where you could find a few human faces in the morning, in the noon and in the evening. But those human beings were completely indifferent about everything in Madhupur. They usually showed neither any excitement nor any exuberance about the place. Each of them was as if engrossed in their own aloofness.

But that day sitting in the waiting room, I kept dreaming so many things about Madhupur. While shuffling through the pages of a detective novel, I could feel that a gentle lady sitting in front and weaving a woollen cloth was looking at me intermittently. There was a strange curiosity in her eyes whereas a thin, wry smile played on her lips. She was perhaps waiting there for a coming train. I no more had the age to enjoy the stare of lady at me in such a calm and secluded place. At an age of above fifty, my dishevelled, greying hairs were flying above my head like 'kasatandi[1]' flowers. While shaving every day, I could see the deepening frowns on my cheek on the mirror. It was a clear testimony of my diminishing youthfulness. These deepening frowns had intensified the roughness of my face.

The gentle lady kept on knitting wool with a downcast head. I kept on shuffling the pages of my detective novel.

If I stayed for two days more in that haunted house in Madhupur, I would have certainly become mad. Two days ago, I met a gentleman in Hotel Parvati. He was a local. I developed an acquaintance with him while taking tea. He told me: "With so many places around, why did you come to Madhupur? No sensible man ever comes to Madhupur anymore. Oh! Do you speak of that judge and that landlord? Those two are thoroughly mad people. They do not come out of their chambers. Two people had gone to the judge's room for 'chanda[2]' for the Jagaddhatri[3] Puja." Wearing a 'lungi[4],' the judge hounded them out with a large stick in his hand."

I thought then I have done well in not going to the esteemed judge's house for a gentle gossip. I had almost reached the gate of his house. But I was discouraged by the

---

1   It is white coloured Indian sub-continental flower.
2   Some monetary contribution.
3   A goddess in Hindu religion.
4   A long-clothed attire for Indian men.

weeded garden and the old, mossy building. I came back as if I had seen a ghost.

The gentleman said again: "Did you not find another house other than 'Madhukunj'? I answered: "A friend of mine from Patna had arranged this house for me. I did not have to pay any rent. Only, I had paid some tips to the watchman."

"O! For that greed you decided to stay there? But after evening, the local people fear moving along its front road." I remembered how strangely the watchman reacted when I handed him the letter given by my Patna friend recommending my stay at 'Madhukunj.' There was a strange reaction in the watchman's tone. He told me: "If you feel any difficulty, please tell me. I can stay in the bungalow for your help. It's an antique and forsaken bungalow. That's why I am telling."

The watchman slept there on the veranda during my stay of four nights in that bungalow. He mostly spent sleepless nights there and I often found him sitting on the bench at midnight. I often asked him: "Why are you sitting instead of sleeping?" He promptly answered: "You are a newcomer. So, I am a little worried about you. But you don't worry. I am always there for your help." I kept thinking that in the greed of some tips, he is showing so much of concern for me. Let him sit there for the whole night. What is my problem?

I asked that gentleman in Hotel Parvati: "Sir! Everybody is afraid of Madhukunj. Is it a haunted house?"

He answered: "A few years ago, an old Bengali lady used to stay in Madhukunj with her daughter-in-law and a few servants. Both were widows. One day, the daughter-in-law bolted the room from inside and committed suicide by hanging herself from the ceiling. After that her mother-in-law left for Brundaban. From that day, the house has been lying vacant like a haunted house. On rare occasions, the mother-in-law's relatives come here and stay for a few days. A lot of people have seen the ghost of the daughter-in-law in moonlit nights. She was found standing denuded on the middle of the street."

But I was someone who never feared ghosts. So the story probably had little impact on my psyche. But perhaps for this reason, the watchman sleeps every night on the veranda burning the lantern. But I thought that the watchman took that risk (suppressing his own fear for ghosts) only in greed for the tips.

But did a human being remain alive after his death? Then how could people see that lady even after her death. This was all rubbish, all rumours and heresies. I never believed in such stupid and meaningless ghost anecdotes. But the gentleman, while dropping the cigarette ashes into the finished tea cup, said: "It's a different matter that you don't believe such stories. But it's a fact that like some memories that always haunt us, there are also some dead human beings that come back to Earth as ghosts. They cannot sever their ties with their previous births. Those that have been able to attain salvation do not of course come back."

"This is another mad man." I said to myself.

I did not argue further with the gentleman.

****

I kept on shuffling the pages of the detective novel in the waiting room.

But the gentle lady was caught this time. She kept on stealthily staring at me and perhaps kept on thinking that I was not catching it as I had buried my face into the pages of the novel. But I knew what she was doing and suddenly I lifted my head and looked straight into her eyes. She could not divert her glance immediately and was caught. Then she gently smiled at me and said: "Can you not recognize me Nikhil Babu? You are Nikhil Chaudhury, right?" But how could the gentle lady know my name? But there was a strange acquaintance in her voice. The same deep chasm in her left cheek when she smiled! I said: "Hey Kalyani! You are here. How strange!" Kalyani was my classmate in college. During our days, women's education had not developed considerably. In our class, there were only two girls. Kalyani said in an artificial-looking sullen voice: "Ok! You did not recognize me, right! You men are like that. You do not take time to forget. You forget even your friends in a moment."

"A moment . . ." I gently retorted. "Thirty/thirty five years are a moment for you?" I said and continued: "How could have I thought that I shall meet you here in this forsaken waiting room after so long? But how come you are alone? Where is your mister . . .?"

A wry smile floated on Kalyani's lips and she said: "I have no mister. I am still Miss Kalyani Das. A Hindi Reader in Mujafarpur Govt. College!"

Now I realized that she was not wearing vermilion on her forehead. In a slightly apprehensive voice, I asked: "Is it due to some vow or for the sake of some spiritual pursuit?"

Kalyani answered: "You can say any of these. But you know that I was never interested in getting entangled in family life."

But how could she know that only for her I had mugged up R. N. Tagore's poem "Kalyani" that day:

In the bower of flowers is thy matchless abode
Oh the harbinger of prosperity!
Thou remain busy in your chores evermore.
I could not remember the following lines.
My friend Kuna parodied these lines:
Alone is your abode in the midst of hawthorn fences
Hey Kalyani!
You are always busy in the History Honours class.

Kalyani stopped knitting wool and started gossiping with me. She said to me: "I can see you have not yet relinquished the habit of shuffling through a book's pages. Do you remember that despite not being a student of History honours, you always used to come to the Library to attend to History seminars? You used to open up the pages of a journal and sit; but I know you did not read a single line from that. You were a student of English Honours."

I had absolutely no idea that Kalyani observed my activities that day with such keenness. Even if our college was a co-education institution, there were hardly eight/ten girl students in the college. Perhaps that is why every girl student had multiple admirers. Not lovers exactly for love is never a one sided affair!

But I was certainly Kalyani's lover. But of course that love remained unexpressed. Firstly, I was always a shy guy, and more so, our society was not at all permissive those days. That is why I could never tell her: "Kalyani! I love you."

I was lost in scrambling these past memories and suddenly, I came to senses and realized that it was no more any occasion for such meaningless, sentimental talks. It was just a mere coincidence that we met after such long time. But we could not also have talked about our families as none of us had them. Neither was it an occasion for political discussions nor any of us was interested in that. If I was a student of History, then I could have perhaps discussed History with her.

But I was a student of English Honours. I used to come to History seminars only to see Kalyani. Even now I can hear the rhythmic sound of my beating heart that day. But my friend Kuna could somehow observe my perennial inability to fall in love and tell me: "Which girl will ever fall in love with a coward like you?" Amongst our contemporaries, Kuna was a famous and established lover. I had seen him regularly receiving blue-coloured love letters from his unknown beloved. Sometimes, I was getting jealous of him. He could easily find a girlfriend for him and I was such a novice in this matter. Kuna told me again: "How can a coward like you ever impress a girl?" But the fact is that I was truly an incorrigibly shy guy. But I had not hesitated to ask Kuna: "Then tell me what can I do to have a girlfriend?" Kuna promptly answered: "You have to be heroic, chivalrous as girls admire heroism and chivalry. If one day you can muster some courage and hold Kalyani's hand in yours and say Kalyani I love you, she would definitely reciprocate."

But I asked Kuna: "If she complains before the principal?"

Kuna promptly responded: "There is risk in everything in life." His words still reverberated in my ears.

The cloudless autumn sky was falling in my eyes through the open window of the waiting room. A light white cloud kept on drifting along the sky like a piece of broken memory. I asked Kalyani: "I have forgotten to ask you your destination. Patna or Hazaribag? Kalyani answered: "I am waiting for 77-Down-North Indian Express. I will be going to Durgapur. My uncle stays there."

I breathed a deep sigh of relief. It was already four o' clock. 77-Down-Madhupur express would arrive at the platform at 5.27 pm. Of course, if it was on the right time! Like the gentleman in Hotel 'Parvati,' seeing the nude lady's ghost on the Madhupur streets in a moonlit night, I was now seeing right before me the ghost of my past. Kalyani's sudden closeness was a strange and inexplicable experience now for me. But how mad I was for such closeness years ago! The sheer thought of it perplexed my mind now. Were we all mere playthings in the hands of destiny? When the background of time changes, also change are our thought and behaviour. This realization came to me abruptly.

I was deeply engrossed in my thoughts when Kalyani interrupted me and said smilingly: "I cannot control my laughter when I remember that day." I answered absentmindedly: "I do not remember any such laughable incident." Then I said to myself: "Your and my histories are tragic ones. Of course now, they might look comic."

But Kalyani had not at all forgotten that incident: "Why were you so nervous that day? Your face that day . . . She started laughing uncontrollably."

"Nervous! When?" I asked in a curious voice.

Kalyani became garrulous and said: "You came that day to the History seminar. You were shuffling through the pages of a journal. That was an archaeological journal and I know that you could not have understood a single word of it. But I could clearly see that you were throwing stealthy glances at me. I could also hear the sound of your deep breathings. And suddenly, you came walking towards me like a storm and out of shame, I buried my face in the History book of Sir Jadunath Sarkar. You asked for a pencil to take a note of something. You had left your pen, and pencil at home. And you desperately wanted to take notes from an archaeological journal. I would clearly see all these were mere pretensions. Without lifting my head from the book, I handed you the pencil. But you wanted to touch my finger instead of the pencil. Your hand was shaking terribly. The pencil fell on the ground. Then you left the place."

Now I remembered that it was my friend Kuna's formula that I wanted to apply to Kalyani that day. I had mustered a lot of courage to press her hand a little hard in the guise of borrowing a pencil and then profess my love to her. But I did not succeed at all in my endeavour. Truly, it was a laughable incident that day. Only Charley Chaplin could have acted perfectly for this scene. But what is the meaning of that incident after so many years of its actual happening?

Without answering anything, I kept on shuffling through the pages of that detective novel.

I was no more interested in recounting the details of that incident. So to divert attention, I said: "Oh! It's very hot and humid today. These people have not even given a fan for this waiting room. But they give long speeches in the name of passenger amenity.

Even Kalyani felt a little shy of having described that incident. She buried her head down and kept knitting wool as if there has not been any conversation between us so far.

Then a bell rang breaking all silence of the waiting room.

The waiting room bearer came in and said: "77-Down is almost arriving. This is the second bell."

I was assured that the train would arrive at last.

Kalyani's soliloquies had now come to an end. But it was a pleasant feeling for meeting someone so close to me after so many years.

Kalyani suddenly extended her right hand towards mine and said: "Please see the lines on my palm and tell me my fortune. You were a great palmist, right?"

"I was practicing palmistry and mesmerism etc. those days. But how could you know that?" I asked Kalyani.

She said: "The way you boys were loitering around us, we also kept track of all information about you people. Apart from that I have so many times seen palmistry books in your hand in those History seminars. Are you a serious palmistry or what?"

I held Kalyani's right palm in my hand and looked carefully at the lines. The lifeline, the fate line, the wealth line . . . But I had truly forgotten the finer arts of palmistry by now. Holding Kalyani's hand in mine was no more a delightful, an exciting and an eclectic experience. I felt so cold and indifferent. It was rather a discomforting feeling that I had while holding her hand. I left it and said: "I have forgotten palmistry long ago, Kalyani. Is it so that a human being's destiny is written only on his/her palms?"

I looked at Kalyani's eyes and could feel that she was a little hurt by my words.

Now, the third bell rang.

Kalyani came out of the platform holding an attaché inn her hand while a yellow vanity bag was dangling from her left arm. Then she said to me: "Ok! Bye! Who knows when we might meet again like this, suddenly?"

I also walked a little distance to say bye to Kalyani. 77-Down waited for three minutes in the platform and left. After a few minutes of commotion, the platform came back to its original stoic silence. My train was to arrive two hours later. There was not even a tea stall in the platform. I walked alongside the railway track for some time absentmindedly, only to get rid of my boredom and aloofness.

The afternoon shade descended onto a 'Palash[5]' tree at a distance. The tree looked to me like a female ghost, a denuded female ghost, like the one the gentleman of Hotel 'Parvati' saw on the Madhupur streets in moonlit nights. Now I saw the denuded female ghost of my past right before me, in broad daylight. But it did not surprise me anymore.

The ghost of my past kept dancing before me and I kept walking . . .

****

---

5   An Indian sub-continental tree with beautiful red flowers. Its botanical name is Butea monosperma.

The Last Redemption

Like the humming of hundreds of flies, sounded the morning chorus of the Buddhist disciples in Grudhrakuta Vihara[6].

"Om namah samasta buddhanang apratihata sasanam."

(We bow before the undefeatable intellectuals.)

On the branches of a tree inside a mango orchard, a cuckoo sang a mating song for its partner." Nilotpala kept listening to it.

Nilotpala was a salvation-seeking Buddhist disciple. He had wilfully relinquished all earthly bondings—love, lust, sensuality, desire . . . How could he then have appreciated the cuckoo's mating song?

Nilotpala said: "Hey stupid bird! I have no interest in your sensual song. Yet, it is regarded as the best symphony in the world of music. What a terrible irony! Your song is the salvation, an unfathomable emptiness where all beings

---

6   Here it refers to a Buddhist monastery.

dissolve. Yet from within this emptiness, does emerge a brimming completeness—the completeness of all beings, all existences.

The cuckoo's song penetrated through the inmost recesses of the mango-orchard, and kept on echoing like the reverberations of an undying desire.

For a moment, Nilotpala forgot his divine chantings, and started listening to the cuckoo's sensual song. Willy-nilly, he was getting attracted.

He looked through the window at the trees' branches in Grudhrakuta-Vihara's mango-orchard; they looked to him like a nude woman's sharp, fleshy limbs spread out against the vast expanses of a golden sky.

Nilotpala concentrated on chanting his divine songs. If he chanted these mantras one lakh and eight times, he would get divine blessings from Lord Buddha.

He had no time thus to imagine a woman's nude limbs in the mango tree's branches in a spring morning. He was a salvation-seeker and as a principle, must have refrained from such impious, worldly imaginings. A herd of Buddhist disciples came towards him while chanting spiritual mantras and listening to them from their mouths was for Nilotpala another step closer to salvation. The usual duty of these salvation-seeking Buddhist disciples was to light candles before the statues of Buddhist gods and goddesses like Abalokiteswara, Pragyanparamita, Amoghasiddhi, Tara, Akhyoba, Lochana etc. placed in the ancient caves, and then to roam from chamber to chamber in Grudhrakuta-Vihara spreading Lord Buddha's divine messages all around.

Nilotpala looked like getting up from a dream. And then he chanted:

"Om namah samasta buddhanang apratihata sasanam."

(We bow before the undefeatable intellectuals.)

The disciples met Nilotpala in his room, lighted the candles with ghee and left. The ambience got heavier with the smell of burnt ghee and wick.

But where was the lady whose anklet's symphony Nilotpala was desperately waiting to hear? Where was Swetaparna's beautiful daughter-in-law?

"Ah Madhubrata!" Thought Nilotpala for a moment.

In that ignited moment in a tranquil night, her memory shook Nilotpala's whole being like a sharp sting of pain.

Forgetting his chantings, he shouted inadvertently: "Madhubrata! Madhubrata!"

Last time, Madhubrata did not come to the sacred ceremony. A few days before, Nilotpala's friend Bajrabahu met her in her abode when he roamed from house to house for begging. That day Madhubrata had offered alms to him in her own hands. But as a principle, a disciple once after collecting alms from a house, was not supposed to visit the same for a stipulated period of time. So, Bajrabahu did not have the liberty to revisit Madhubrata's in the immediate future.

Nilotpala shouted: "Ah! Madhubrata!"

Madhubrata's pair of tormented eyes flashed for a moment in his memory and vanished. They looked like two half-bloomed lotuses in a still-water pond and delicately sparkled like dew dew-drops in soft grass.

"Om namah samasta buddhanang..." Chanted Nilotpala.

Another Cuckoo's sensuous mating song was heard. It silenced his chantings.

Nilotpala felt like asking his guru Acharya[7] Santideva about what really is eternal? This cuckoo's desperate mating song? Or the chantings of divine mantras?

He felt that every argument, every divine chanting becomes silent one day; but the bird's sensuous mating song remains eternal.

"Then why should one relinquish every earthly pleasure and enjoyment and indulge in self-abnegation and then, venture into salvation?" Nilotpala asked himself.

There were two red-granite statues placed inside an ancient grove in Nilotpala's chamber. The statues were of Abalokiteswara and Pragyanparamita, both in meditation, but in tight embrace. Some disciple had placed at their feet a few clusters of 'Ashokamanjari[8]' flowers. Pragyanparamita's breasts were pressed against Abalokiteswara's chest. On both their faces was a deep sense of contentment.

The night had become silent. The inmates of the 'Vihara,' after confessing their sins and mistakes before Acharya Santideva, went happy and contented to their rooms and slept.

But Acharya Santideva was still meditating on a seat outside his room in a building's third storey in Grudhrakuta Vihara. In the night's flooding moonlight, he looked like an immovable stone effigy. In the spreading moonlight,

---

7   An ancient name for a Guru.
8   A red-coloured flower that blooms in the Indian subcontinent. Its botanical name is Saraca Asoka.

the shades of the orchard's mango trees looked like dark patches scattered on Earth. A tattler bird screamed restlessly as if to awaken the night sleeping like an innocent virgin.

At Nilotpala's call, Santideva opened his eyes, and looked into the darkness of the shade. Acharya Santidev knew so far that Nilotpala was one amongst the best disciples in the whole 'Vihara' in terms of maintaining sacredness, self-abnegation, and spiritual perseverance. He could not imagine that even he might be having some worldly fallibility like this.

He therefore asked: "Hey Nilotpala! What makes you come to me in the middle of the night?"

Nilotpala could not provide an abrupt answer and kept quiet for some time. His voice was as if choking for an honest confession.

He finally admitted in an unambiguous voice: "I have fallen in love with disciple Swetaparna's daughter-in-law Madhubrata. Madhubrata was married to the former's son Nalinakshya who, after their first night, went on a trading-voyage across the sea with a few fellow-voyagers. It was a few years ago and from that day onwards he is never seen again. Some of Pataliputra[9]'s traders who have returned home from their voyages across beyond-the-sea islands say that he has been killed by sea-pirates. Some others say that he has started a new life with an unknown lady in a foreign island. Swetaparna, after prolonged and fortuitous waiting for his son's return, has finally accepted that he is dead and hence, has completed all essential, religious death-rites for his son. Everybody has accepted that Nalinakshya is dead. Yet, Madhubrata is living with a futile expectation that he

---

9   The capital city of the ancient city of Magadha.

will come back one day—a hope that is alive like the un-extinguished wick of a candle."

****

A soft autumn afternoon! As per the usual practice, Nilotpala after finishing his meal in disciple Swetaparna's room, was planning to move out before dusk. Madhubrata accosted him through her chamber's window: "Nilotpala!" (Nilotpala felt the soft, pleasing touch of her blushful voice along with her bracelet and anklets' sweet symphony deep within his soul. It was beautiful, enchanting like the cuckoo's tender, mellifluous singing in the mango orchard, like the soothing twitter of the tattler bird in the tranquil, moonlit sky.)

Before Nilotpala, appeared the blue-gown-clad, the flower-embedded, the slim-figured, the dusky-complexioned, and the beautiful Madhubrata. Her dye-ridden feet were full of a musical symphony. Her slim, supple figure was lascivious, enticing. But her eyes that looked like inverted lotus leaves were filled with the stoic indifference of a shadowy lake. Nilotpala was mesmerized.

Nothing but the incessant hooting of the pigeons busy lovemaking in the sty was audible in that languorous afternoon.

With the touch of Madhubrata's deep breath on his skin, Nilotpala got back to his senses. He looked into the enormous depths of her eyes. Her face was almost washed by a few tear-drops fallen from her lotus-eyes. Her softened lips looked vibrating with a question.

Nilotpala asked with a sympathetic voice: "What would you ask me, dear?"

Madhubrata stretched her left palm towards Nilotpala and asked in a blushful voice: "Can you look at my palm and prognosticate whether my husband whom I had said adieu with the setting sun over River Ganga will return or not? He has left me after our first night and has never returned then."

Nilotpala held Madhubrata's left palm in his hands like a hypnotized man. Palm-telling was indeed a prohibited art for the Buddhist disciples and thus, it was not possible for him to answer her questions. Yet, he kept on holding her soft, spongy left palm in his hands in that mesmeric afternoon. It seemed as if his hungry nerves and tendons were rejuvenated with a new life, a new sensation. Nilotpala felt like getting lost in a trance. It seemed as if his whole existence was getting dissolved in a fathomless vacuum. He felt that the profound emptiness that he had been searching for years through deep meditations and had not yet gotten was achieved in this captivating moment, in Madhubrata's supple touch in this dusky, pigeon-infested afternoon. His whole being was thoroughly shaken up.

"This is the great, inexplicable emptiness in which everything dissolves—body and soul, flesh and appearance, everything. This touch is the greatest pleasure through which the body transforms into the bodiless. This is salvation." Thought Nilotpala! The profound happiness that was visible on Abalokiteswara and Pragyanparamita's faces was also felt by him in that moment.

His deep, warm breath was as if burning Madhubrata's soft, delicate palm. She slowly dragged it back from Nilotpala's hands and hid it in her saree[10]. Her eyes slowly closed down beneath her descending brows.

---

10   A typical long-clothed attire that Indian women wear.

Nilotpala got back to his senses, but Madhubrata had left by now. His wakeful trance was gradually coming to an end in the midst of the pigeons' relentless hooting inside the sty.

****

Sanitdeva sat in his meditational posture as usual. The tattler bird's frenzied shouting had made everybody realize the moonlit night's immense tranquillity and loneliness.

Nilotpala told Santideva: "Hey guru! The day Madhubrata touched me, I have lost all control over myself. My body's desire has gotten reignited and has undermined my pursuit for divinity. But O Guru! In that touch of the moment I have realized salvation, that eternal emptiness we all are searching for. Is that realization false, Gurudev[11]?"

Santideva was sitting like a meditating Buddha. Nilotpala's questions reverberated in his ears like the tattler bird's sharp cry in the tranquilized night-sky.

He answered: "Nilotpala! Tathagata[12] has found the panacea for suffering. The cycle is like this: "Thirst from beauty, pain from thirst and suffering from pain! So, to get rid of pain and suffering, you need to conquer your thirst, your sensual desire. Now conquering desire is salvation— liberation from the cycle of birth and death."

Explaining this, Santideva got back to his meditation. Nilotpala stood like an immovable shadow along the wall. The restless tatter bird climbed higher up into the sky and then, descended into the shades of the mango groove like an unsatisfied, thirsty soul and then, kept on traversing across the night's excited nerves like an unstoppable whim,

---

11   A respectable term for teacher.
12   Another name for Lord Buddha.

an irrepressible desire. It climbed up again and then, circled the moonlit sky weaving shifting patterns of hundreds of waves in its vast, sprawling vacuum.

The night's moonlight spread across the sky like the unfastened dresses of the denuded Urvashi[13]. Nilotpala was lost in the hypnotic allure of that flooding moonlight. Tathagata has said: "Beauty is the cause of grief; it is a hindrance to salvation." But this beauty gave Nilotpala pleasure, not pain—the beauty of this moonlit night, the beauty of Madhubrata, the softness of her palm! They were beautiful, enchanting, enticing. In that touch, Nilotpala felt the infinite pleasures of salvation. But of course, this pleasurable moment was transient; it came, embraced him and disappeared.

Nilotpala's desire for more of Madhubrata's proximity was getting ignited like a volcanic eruption. It was burning the cool, tranquil moonlight into ashes.

Santideva told him in a cold and calculated voice: "Son! It's late in the night. Now you go and sleep. But as a step towards the attainment of salvation, you have to spend three weeks inside the crematorium from tomorrow onwards."

Nilotpala came back from the 'Vihara' into his chamber. The candle below Abalokiteswara and Pragyanparamita's statues had gotten extinguished long before. A thin ray of moonlight had scattered almost imperceptibly on the chamber's stone-floor. The tattler bird's restless shout in the night sky kept him waking till late in the night. He was mesmerized by the smell of the mango buds.

****

---

13   A heavenly nymph in Indian mythology known for her beauty.

That day while returning to his place, Tathagata was taking rest with his disciples in a Sal-forest at the outskirts of the Malla[14] community's village. It was springtime and its joyous atmosphere had spread through the whole forest like his heavenly blessings. From within the forest's enormous depths, a cuckoo's desperate song was as if calling the former to wake up from its sleep. The song created an upheaval along the Sal-forest's branches and leaves while the ceaseless humming of the jungle-bees added to the noise.

At this point, the thought of women disturbed disciple Ananda's mind who asked Tathagata: "God! What should be the relation between women and the disciples?"

Tathagata answered: "Every disciple's duty is to stay away from women."

Ananda asked: "Hey God! But what if some beautiful lady comes your way some time?"

Tathagata answered: "Then you have to control yourself by subduing the fickleness of your senses."

Ananda asked again: "Then what will be relationship between the disciples and women?"

Tathagata answered: "The disciples must refrain from verbal interactions with them."

Ananda asked again: "If a lady starts interacting with a disciple?"

Tathagata answered: "then quietly go away from her with a downcast head."

****

---

14   An ancient Buddhist community.

The last rays of the moon setting high up in the distant horizon came through the open door of Madhubrata's chamber and fell on her tormented pair of eyes that were slowly getting closed. The still night's plaintive wind was as if getting burnt with her long breaths.

Nilotpala got up from his stone-bed and closed the doors of his chamber.

II

A long, sprawling crematorium lied stretched on the shade-less, shrub-less top of the Grudhrakuta Mountain. On that ground, Nilotpala was desperately searching for something in the midst of the congregated human bones, skeletons, skulls and the tattered dresses, as if the mystery of the whole creation laid concealed in that mess. Without shave, his head was full of long hairs whereas his chin was covered with a huge beard. His sparkling, bright face looked pale and wrinkled and his shrunk skin looked hard and lifeless like dry flesh. His ochre-coloured dress looked banal, without any noticeable grandeur or sophistication. He was wearing an abandoned dress as an undergarment. His eyes were sunken deep into their sockets and looked blood-red in colour.

Guru Santideva's orders were clear and unambiguous: "As long as Nilotpala does not conquer his desire and his senses, he can never be a complete Buddhist disciple." Nilotpala had till now not been able to do that. His desire for beauty and the thirst for the body still persisted in his subconscious. That is why on the orders of Acharya Santideva and as a norm for the salvation-seekers, he was sent to this crematorium to practice self-abnegation through meditation.

All these salvation-seeking individuals had to go through the same process of self-abnegation in the crematorium so that they could realize the transience of this body of flesh and bones which will ultimately perish in the crematorial fire. So, this momentary desire for physical beauty is nothing but a futile illusion. Nothing shall remain permanently; this beautiful body shall also perish one day. This realization was of utmost importance for someone who was on the pursuit of salvation. A triumph over beauty, desire and grief ws the pathway to salvation and Nilotpala was to master this craft in the crematorium.

On the burnt valley of the noon, the cool shade of the mountain-range came down like a soothing balm. At the outer edge of the crematorium, a herd of vultures came flying from the dead branches of a lightening-burnt tree sniffing a corpse somewhere nearby. The vultures descended at some distance and started rubbing their beaks against the ground. Nilotpala thought that some corpse was lying out there and hence, ran towards it. The vultures still remained unperturbed and were heedless of Nilotpala's menacing approach. Nilotpala lifted a stone and threw at them so as to drive them away from the body.

Someone had placed a corpse beneath the cover of a stone. Nilotpala lifted the stone in both his hands so as to have a look.

A grief-stricken father had placed his toddler's tender body on a carefully prepared bed of leaves such that it would not be damaged by the rough touch of the pebbly and rugged soil. He had placed near the body a colourful toy ... the baby's playmate. Oh! This child looked like a soft, delicate flower fallen from its stem. It was heartrending for Nilotpala to look at his face.

Nilotpala never had any sense of attachment with any child previously, neither did he have any feeling for them. But this time he wanted to lift the tender baby in his arms. But then he stepped back at the sight of a poisonous snake nearby. A blue colour had spread through the baby's skin. His tender lips had turned black.

Nilotpala cried with a grief-stricken voice: "O God! I cannot bear this sight. The baby has turned into a green corpse. It's unbearable God! It's unbearable."

Nilotpala shouted again: "This body! This body! It's beautiful and powerful for only a few days. Then... Then... A day comes when it becomes food for dogs and jackals and vultures, then for worms and germs... Then... Then...

Nilotpala lifted his hands into the vast expanses of the sky and shouted: "Then . . . Then . . ."

His words hit the mountains around the empty ravine and echoed: "Then . . . Then . . ."

Then he said: "It's then a congregation of scattered bones, of pounded bones . . . Nothing else."

In his frenzied imagination, Nilotpala saw Tathagata telling Ananda in that Sal-jungle: "These colourless bones are the ultimate consequences of your desire for beauty, your hunger for flesh . . ."

Nilotpala started shouting like a mad man: "Bones . . . Bones . . ."

Then he lifted his muscular arms into the air and shouted at himself: "Nilotpala! These are not your muscular arms. These are a pair of dry, desiccated bones. Nilotpala! You yourself are a colourless, worm-infested bone."

But then why would a piece of bone seek salvation?

Nilotpala looked at the sky and shouted: "Can you tell the sky what is the need for salvation for this piece of bone? This piece of bone does not have another birth! It won't come back; it does not have a desire for flesh; it does not have either discontent or grief . . . It's only a piece of bone. Only a piece of bone!"

Then it's all salvation . . . Great happiness. An absolute liberation from the cycle of birth and death!"

The gloomy shade of the mountain-covered ravine condensed into the tranquillity of the surrounding. A deep commotion from the Earth's tormented soul painted the horizon with a sprawling, reddish hue.

On the other side of the crematorium, another group of corpse-carriers were returning across the murky, crimson light of the dusk.

The task of self-abnegation in the crematorium entrusted to Nilotpala by Santideva has been completed. Nilotpala has now understood the mystery behind birth and death and thus, the futility of this earthly life, of this body with its meaningless beauty and sensual appeal. The beauty and sensuality of a woman's body can no more entrap him; they can no more arouse in him the primitive demon of desire. Today, Nilotpala is liberated from the incarcerations of desire and the thirst for body; he is liberated like an arrow unleashed from a bow. Now he can get back into his confined meditation chamber of 'Grudhrakuta Vihara' with a happy and contented disposition.

The spring has lost most of its beauty and grandeur.

From the burnt out bed of spring, summer is rising vigorously with its ruthless and burning blood-red eyes.

Today Acharya Santideva will coronate Nilotpala with the accolade of being a true Buddhist disciple. After that, Nilotpala will be Kalyanamitra[15] Acharya Nilotpala.

He no more has to sit beside a corpse and watch the pantomime of life disappearing into the flames of death, step by step. Today all his perseverance has come to an end. Today is the most auspicious occasion of his life. Nilotpala suddenly remembered: "Today is a full moon night."

A new corpse had entered into the crematorium. Nilotpala could not resist his desire of having a look at it. Like a wild animal sniffing the prey, he moved towards the corpse with slow and measured steps.

In a secluded corner of the thorny shrub-infested crematorium, the corpse-carriers had kept a blue-attire-clad body beneath the cover of a few stones. Nilotpala lifted these stones in both his hands.

It was a woman's corpse lying on the ground. Except her face, her whole body was covered with one blue attire. Oh! A woman! A woman! A burning flame! In the frozen darkness of the crematorium, it was lying abandoned— cold and stiffened.

Nilotpala rubbed his sunken eyes and looked at the body placed in the graveyard's shaded groove.

Gosh! It was Swetaparna's daughter-in-law Madhubrata.

The same Madubrata whose beauty had become a hindrance to his salvation-seeking endeavour! Nilotpala was irresistibly enamoured by her beauty and had to come to the crematorium to stay away from her so that she no

---

15   A title that authenticates someone as a successful Buddhist disciple.

more remained a hindrance to his spiritual pursuit. But she has followed him even after his death. For Nilotpala, to confront her was like digging an old wound. To get rid of his attraction towards her, Nilotpala had roamed across the crematorium like a ghost, scrambling corpses after corpses, to know the mystery behind the cycle of birth and death. But today, his tormented past has come back again to meet him, to confront him; it has stuck to him like an unbreakable shadow.

In a moment, all his perseverance, all his spiritual endeavours disappeared like the gentle breeze of spring.

The same blue-attire-clad, slim-figured Madhubrata! It seemed as if she was looking at him, with her lotus-eyes, with her dilated eyebrows. Her reddish lips were open and inviting for a union. There was a blushful expression on her face.

Like a hungry, wild animal, Nilotpala took off the dresses from her body in both his hands.

He held her nude, lifeless body in tight embrace while feeling its sensuous touch on his own. They were becoming one; they were merging into each other, just like Abalokiteswara and Pragyanparamita in those statues in his chamber. Nilotpala started kissing every part of her body vigorously like a lunatic. He covered her denuded body with his kisses. He was going mad. He was losing himself in her.

Nilotpala had no idea that Acharya Santideva was already standing behind him, neither was he interested in any way to know that. He was lost in his mad passions.

Acharya Santideva shouted in an angry voice: "Nilotpala! Nilotpala!"

Nilotpala did not answer. He just held Madhubrata's nude, lifeless body in tight embrace on his chest, kissing her frantically across her neck and face.

Santideva shouted again; "What the hell are you doing Nilotpala? What are you doing, you moron, you senseless fellow? What are you doing?"

Nilotpala neither looked at Santideva nor was he disturbed by his presence.

He was lost in true salvation.

Over the mountain range, the luxurious moon was soaring high up into the night sky like a wingless eagle. Nilotpala lifted Madhubrata onto his shoulder and started running deliriously into the darkness of the grooves.

Santideva was helplessly shouting from behind; "Nilotpala! Nilotpala!"

In the empty ravines of the mountain range, Santideva's shout was getting echoed and ricocheted towards him like a crude and biting sarcasm from the mountains.

Holding the nude and dead Madhubrata over his shoulder, Nilotpala was progressively getting lost in the darkness of the grooves.

****

The Imprisoned Father

At the hill's summit, there existed a small prison house; it had a tiny hole through which the morning sunlight poured in and lightened its enormous dark space. The din and bustle of the citizenry was clearly audible from the main road.

Through the hole, the prisoner threw a hungry look at the immense profusion of light outside. It was the morning's quiet and bright ray of light, just like the blessing of Lord Buddha.

Being old and exposed to relentless atrocities, the prisoner looked haggard, hungry and scraggy like a ghost. The wide chest that he once possessed and flaunted with valour was now covered with pale, gray-white hairs. His skin had slackened.

The prisoner was Magadha king Bimbisara.

On the orders of his son Ajatasatru, he had been imprisoned here under this living tomb.

Ajatasatru has vowed to kill him—to kill him by hunger.

In enormous exhaustion and depression, Bimbisara's two sunken eyelids closed down again and his limbs were getting paralysed in extreme hunger. Bimbisara dragged his thirsty tongue over his desiccated lips and screamed in a choked voice—a scream that reverberated inside the prison house like the sharp cry of pain of a haunted-down lion.

This palace was once built in his order. Today in its dark, dingy chamber and away from his loyal citizens, he felt the excruciating pangs of death every moment. These were the punishments for his misdeeds in the previous birth—he thought.

A huge fire once broke out in his earlier capital Kusagranagara. Almost the whole city turned into debris. Bimbisara ordered that the person whose house shall catch fire shall be exiled. But strange was the law of Nature. His own palace caught fire. The king accepted self-imposed exile in 'Seetalabana'.

He was mesmerized by the exquisite scenic beauty of this place that was situated in the banks of river 'Sarpini' and was surrounded by mountains like 'Bipulagiri,' 'Baibharagiri' and 'Grudhrakuta.' By his orders, here was built the new capital city of Magadha—Rajagruha.

Bimbisara lifted his tired, comatose pair of eyes to have a last look at Rajagruha—the eyes that had turned into a pair of stones—lifeless and visionless.

That day when Ajatasatru imprisoned his father Bimbisara, the former's grief-stricken, shrivelled-haired and tearful mother pleaded for mercy before her son:

"Son Ajatasatru."

Ajatasatru answered in a taunting voice: "Give orders Your Excellency, the princess of Kashi[16]".

---

16   Ajatasatru's mother Koshala Devi was the princess of the king-
      dom of Kashi.

"Is it such a shameful thing for you to call me your mother, son?" Said the mother.

"Son! Ha-Ha-Ha! Ajatasatru laughed boisterously and then said in a cruel and gravelly voice: "I do not shy away from calling you my mother. But can you please explain to me what will be the son's reply to a mother who once contemplated to kill him for the fear that one day that son might turn out to be his father's murderer?"

Koshala Devi answered in a helpless voice: "I have told you hundreds of times son that this is nothing but a rumour."

Ajatasatru said: "There is no smoke without fire, princess of Kashi. But why this discussion? I am ready to accept all your requests except the one that relates to Bimbisara's release."

Koshala Devi wiped away her tears in her saree and told: "Ok fine! If your coronation shall be at the expense of your father's blood, then who can resist? But I have only one request, king. Bimbisara never appreciated any dish except the one prepared by me. Today I want to serve him food in the prison. Please do not deny me this small pleasure of mine."

Ajatasatru said: "Ok! I grant your request."

But after Koshala Devi departed, the king ordered his prison guard Chanda: "The prisoner must not touch the food served to him by Koshala Devi."

****

Almost empty was the water pot. Bimbisara held it in his violently shaking hands and tried to touch it with his lips. It fell and broke into splinters. The morning sun had soared high up into the sky. The thin ray of light that entered the dark room through the hole had also disappeared. In the dark, dingy and foul-smelling chamber of the prison house, reigned nothing but the brooding, cruel atmosphere of death.

Hunger no more tortured Bimbisara. What remained were only thirst and a tormenting sense of aloofness. "Now, I shall be liberated from that also"—thought the king. "Then it will all be a profound emptiness—like Buddha's meditation. The eyelids will be still." He was murmuring to himself. It was a few moments of silence then. The circle of emptiness was slowly closing on him. But suddenly in his blurring vision, floated the statute of the meditating Lord Buddha spread out against the vast expanses of the limitless sky. The peace and tranquillity in his half-closed eyes were abundant.

Due to excessive thirst, Bimbisara's tongue and lips had started bleeding with droplets of dark, red blood. That blood quenched his thirst to an extent. In a choked voice, he shouted like a wounded animal.

In his diminishing vision, Bimbisara saw floating on the firmament of the sky the Saptaparni ravine of the Grudhrakuta Mountain. One day he was perplexed by the news that the Sakya dynasty's prince Gautama has become a monk and is meditating there. It was a dusky evening with a cloudless sky when Bimbisara, flanked by his royal officials, went to meet Gautama in Grudhrakuta. Gautama was delivering sermons to some of his disciples in Saptaparni. In a garden on the foothills of the mountain, the female peacocks enjoyed the dance of their male counterparts and kissed them through their beaks in an ecstasy of love and mutual adoration. In the nearby grassland, innumerable deers roamed with unbounded joy and excitement. At a distance, a female deer looked at its own reflection in a pond's crystal-clear water and was lost in the secret appreciation of her own beauty.

Buddha was deeply immersed in his meditation; his limbs were resplendent with divine light. There was the calm repose of the dusk in his half-closed eyes and his half-folded palms emanated peaceful blessings for tormented mankind. Bimbisara asked in a temperate voice: "What grief brings you to this deep meditation, prince?"

Gautama smiled gently and answered: "No grief drives me here, Your Excellency! In fact, I am in search for its cause and its remedy."

Bimbisara laughed loudly and said: "The remedy is very simple, prince. But how would you get it in these deserted ravines of Saptaparni? Come then to the celebration hall of Rajagruha. You will get all your answers in the brimming wine and voluptuous women of Magadha."

Bimbisara laughed loudly again in luxuriant ecstasy. Gautama's two half-closed eyelids got heavier like the evening's approaching darkness and started closing down.

****

Ah! The thirst is tearing apart Bimbisara's windpipe.

****

After a few moments' silence, Gautama spoke: "The remedy of this thirst is not in the desire, king. It is in the relinquishment of desire."

****

The deathlike silence of the prison house's closed compartment echoed with those words.

****

The Magadha ladies danced no more; their iron-chained, dyed feet had become silent; the gloom of death had filled their collyrium-ridden eyes. In the brimming wine pots, there were dancing the murderous bubbles of venom.

****

"Whose anklet's symphony do I hear? Koshala Devi? The queen?" Bimbisara said to himself.

The guards of the prison were changing. The sound of the iron armour was faintly heard. In unbearable thirst, Bimbisara bit one of his arms like an injured wild animal.

2

Through the window, Ajatasatru kept looking at the spreading mountain ranges outside without a blink in his eyes. On the cot was sleeping like a dead river his pregnant wife Bajra. From the pigeon sty, many pigeons were flying away and then, coming back. A peacock in the garden was spreading its tail madly in a dance.

Bajra called in a slow voice: "King!"

While sitting on the cot near her, Ajatasatru softly dragged his palm on her pale forehead and told: "Tell me queen."

Bajra held one of Ajatasatru's hands in tight embrace and told: "Tell me king whether this will be a son or a daughter?"

Ajatasatru was startled a little by her question.

Bajra continued with her same, cruel question: "Tell me king whether this will be a son or a daughter?"

Ajatasatru got up from her bed and went inside his secret chamber without uttering a single word. Bajra screamed with an unbearable pain.

In the blurred vision of Ajatasatru, floated the darkness of the Rajagruha prison house like an enigma, a curse.

So cruel was that 'future-tell!' Bajra's first son shall kill his father. The expressions became harder on Ajatasatru's stony face. Would he imprison the pregnant queen and throw her in the dark chambers of the prison house? Would he throw the newborn baby into the unfathomable depths of the dark well? Was it so impossible for him to destroy both his past and his future in his own hands? The past was already imprisoned inside the prison house. What about the future? But his 'present' was getting torn between his 'past' and his 'future.' All these conflicting thoughts started weighing heavily on him.

Bajra's screams were largely audible. The pains of pregnancy! The embryo wanted to manifest, tearing apart her uterus.

Ajatasatru heard someone's footstep in his closed chamber and hence, looked back. The prison guard Chanda stood before him, as if waiting for further orders.

Ajatasatru asked: "What is the news Chanda?"

Chanda answered: "For the last three days the prisoner has not even been offered water. Today is the fourth day."

Ajatasatru's facial expressions became cruder. He asked Chanda in a rough voice: "Then what?"

Chanda said: "Your Excellency! I could hear the scream—Hey Son! Hey Rajagruha!"

******

From the queen's chamber came the sounds of conches and celebrations. Bajra's screams had become silent long ago. The maid Basumati came in with hastened steps and told: "Good news King. The queen has given birth to a son. You may summon the minister and tell him to arrange for royal celebrations in Rajagruha."

Chanda said: "Give the orders king. Give the orders."

Ajatasatru once looked at the maid Basumati, then again at Chanda. Then like a mad man, he started running outside. Chambers after chambers, steps after steps, streets after streets—Ajatasatru was running like an unstoppable lunatic. He reached at the entrance of the prison house. The guards saluted him.

He ordered: "Open the door, guard."

The two huge iron doors opened with a crackling sound. The atmosphere inside was terribly dark and sinister. Crossing the greyish steps, Ajatasatru frantically ran towards the murky chambers of the prison house.

Today, the father has understood the meaning of fatherhood.

The creator is always benevolent and merciful. Like a baby, Ajatasatru would go and fall at his father's feet, to apologize, to beg for mercy.

But he was a little too late. Bimbisara's lifeless

body laid there on the floor. He had chewed one arm in unbearable hunger, like a wild animal injured with the hunter's arrows. A few drops of blood had flown from the injury and had dried up.

From the palace the relentless blowing of conches was audible signalling the birth of the prince.

****

The Cursed Courtesan

The Lichhabbi[17]-union's conference refectory in Baisali did not have space even for a grain that day. It was jam-packed. Starting from every common man, royal person, intellectual, businessman—everybody had assembled to listen to the judgement on Amrapalli[18].

In such gatherings on other occasions, all the members of the commoners' union were not usually present simultaneously. But today everybody had occupied their respective position on the instructions of the convener.

The speaker got up from his seat to stop the noise and said: "Please listen to me, respected members. There is no need to maintain quorum today. Because as far as I can see, almost all the members of the Licchabbi community are present here. Therefore I request the chief whip to start the proceedings." At the instructions of the speaker, the chief whip Deepankara got up from his seat and said: "Esteemed speaker and all the respected members of the committee.

---

17   It's a clan that lived in the ancient Indian kingdom of Magadha.
18   Amrapalli was a beautiful lady of Magadha during 500 BC (roughly) who had to turn into a public whore under certain circumstances as described in the story. She ultimately became Lord Buddha's disciple.

May I kindly have your attention? Before listening to the judgement on Amrapalli, please listen to her life story from the gardener Asitabarna."

Asitabarna stood up, looked at the assembled people and said: "I am the caretaker of the mango orchard at the outskirts of Baisali[19]. Today, I remember an event of sixteen years ago. It was not yet morning. The collective twitter of the morning birds got me up from bed. The reddish sun was just beginning to bloom in the eastern sky. The wind had gotten heavier with the fragrance of the mango buds. I suddenly heard the cry of a newborn baby. I had been childeless all my life and had always longed for a child. I wonder was it a game of destiny? I remember that day vividly even today. Below a mango tree, some destitute lady had left this beautiful baby. Even her umbilical cord was not severed. Without thinking anything, I lifted her onto my lap. I did not care whether she was the blasphemous child of some whore or even a curse to mankind; I just accepted her as my child. Sixteen years later, today she is your Amrapalli."

Deepankar left his seat, got up and said: "That Amrapalli is today Baisali's terror. Sixteen years ago, this living curse of Baisali was born in a dark moment of a spring night."

Ganadhara asked: "But where is Amrapalli?"

Suddenly the music of Ambapalli's anklet was heard outside the palace. Unclear voices rose from amongst the assembled crowd: "Here is Amrapalli. Here is Amrapalli."

Amrapalli was blue-bodied; her soft feet were dyed with reddish hue in a design that looked like the scattered congregation of pomegranate seeds; her thin waist was

---

19   An ancient Indian city.

covered with a golden string that fell up to her thighs; her arms and breasts were decorated with golden jewelleries; below her curved eyelids were two drunken deer-eyes; they looked like the string of Madana's[20] bent bow.

Deepankara said: "The republic of Baisali lies endangered only for this Amrapalli. States like Bideha, Malla and Kalama are all madly after this cursed beauty. The enormous wealth of this poor gardener's daughter can even ridicule Baisali's huge royal exchequer. If our secret information is correct, the Magadha king Bimbisara plans to abduct her into his palace. Everybody of us would know that it's not entirely impossible for a lecher like Bimbisara. If that turns out to be true, then a military conflict between Baisali and Magadha is inevitable for Baisali would definitely resist such mean attitude by this usurper. But of course, its consequences are also well known. For how long Baisali's small military establishment would sustain itself in front of the might of the gigantic Magadha army? So, it is my sincere request to all of you that as per the customs of the land, let Amrapalli be declared a public-whore before all. For the finalization of this proposal, I ask for a common vote."

Like a deer afraid of the hunter, Amrapalli looked at the assembled citizens. At this point in time, another member Silabhadra got up and said: "This voting is not required as this proposal is unanimously acceptable to all; I believe even Amrapalli won't oppose it."

Thus there was no need for formal voting. The proposal was unanimously accepted through mass clapping by the members.

---

20   Madana is the God of love and lust in Indian mythology.

The speaker got up at this point in time and said: "Esteemed members of the union. With your permission, I declare that Amrapalli henceforth becomes a public-whore. Her beauty is her crime."

2

During the time, which is represented in this narration, this was the custom in states ruled by the communities like Shakya, Koliya, Bideha, Maurya, Buli, Kalama and Bhaga etc. The virgin whose beauty would give rise to conflicts between different states shall ultimately become the public whore. As per this rule, Amrapalli was declared a public-whore in Baisali. But yet, she was still a memorable, intellectual lady of the Buddhist times. In *Theri Gatha*[21], there is present a tearful, autobiographical anecdote written by her describing the deplorable plight of a public whore. It tells the poignant story of how that day, Amrapalli had sacrificed all the pleasures of her life for Baisali—the pleasures of her womanhood, the pleasures of her motherhood, the hopes of her life, her happiness—everything.

The public whores during those times were not simply sex objects for men; they also possessed the highest level of competency in literature, music and dance. In addition, they were unimaginably affluent in a way that it could ridicule the affluence of kings. In the Buddhist text *Binayapittaka*, it is narrated that the whore named "Ardhakashi" of the city of Kashi had an income in one night that would equal the king's revenue for one day. But since she could not get customers at such a high price, she had halved her

---

21   An ancient Buddhist text containing autobiographical poems by women poets.

price. Thus, from that day onwards, she became known as "Ardhakashi."

3

Amrapalli's bedroom in her palace in Baisali! She was lying half-conscious in labour pain on her cot. Her maidservant Sirima stood beside her with a newborn baby in her lap, and intended to say something to Amrapalli.

Sirima called: "Elder sister."

Amrapalli slightly opened her tired eyes and said in a harsh voice: "Why are you standing there Sirima? Go and throw that baby on the roadside. It will be morning after a while."

Sirima told: "What a beautiful, princely baby! It looks exactly like King Bimbisara. I don't feel like throwing him away, elder sister."

Amrapalli's fallen and tortured motherhood was as if raising its head again. Sirima told in a soft voice: "Take the child onto your lap, elder sister. Take the child onto your lap."

Amrapalli shouted like a trampled serpent: "No! No! That's a blasphemous child. He is an incarceration for me. A curse of this life! Go and throw him out right now, Sirima. I would have kept her if she was a girl child. But it's a baby boy. Go and throw him away. I don't want to listen to your arguments anymore."

The baby started crying on Sirima's lap. Amrapalli started shouting: "Press the cloth in his mouth Sirima. Let him be finished. Why do you stand here? Go."

Sirima pressed the baby closer to her breast and left. Amrapalli felt like taking revenge on herself for an abandoned and neglected life.

But why were these streaming tears flooding her eyes? She could not have been so weak, so vulnerable, so emotional. After all, she was a public whore.

4

That day's abandoned child later on went on to become a famous Ayurvedic[22] doctor—Gautama Buddha's disciple, Jeebaka. But there is of course no chronological record in History that tells the growth of this abandoned, nameless, parentless, helpless child of Baisali into a famous doctor in the hands of a childless man.

5

Many years later...

Amrapalli's whorehouse remained empty and people-less. The fresh stems of her spring-tree like body that once was filled with the noise of the lechers, had now dried up. They had left for younger Amrapallis. Amrapalli was now sick with an incurable disease; she was paralyzed. In her dancing feet, there was now the lifelessness of rocks; in her golden body, there was now spreading the darkness of death. A cataract had invaded her deer-eyes. In this scenario, Padmabati was now Baisali's new public whore. Where ever you went, you heard only praises for Padmabati, as if there was no Amrapalli ever in that region.

---

22 An ancient medical practice in India involving the treatment of diseases through herbs and other arborescent materials as medicines.

6

On the sick bed, lied Amrapalli's diseased, dirty body like a lifeless thing. Jeebaka was sitting beside her and was rubbing some balm on her eyelids. Amrapalli shouted like a mad woman in painful voice and told Jeebaka: "Give me some poison Jeebaka. I don't need this life. I know Jeebaka my lost youth won't come back again; my lost vision shall not come back again. Your efforts are futile, Jeebaka. Your efforts are all futile."

Jeebaka rubbed his hand softly on her forehead and said: "Be quiet mother. I assure you I shall bring back your lost health and youth."

The Ayurvedic doctor Jeebaka had a wonderful ability. His words never turned out to be false. In that confidence, Amrapalli had completely surrendered herself to him. What a solace! What calmness! There was wonder in his hands. What affection in this utterance of the word 'mother'! Amrapalli wanted to have a look at him with her blinded eyes. But everything was hazy, like fog. She remembered the day when she felt the joys of motherhood while holding that newborn baby in her breasts; the same joy she felt today with the touch of Jeebaka's calm, soothing hands.

Amrapalli asked; "Who are you Jeebaka?"

Jeebaka answered: "I am a beggar, mother. I am a beggar. Without being perturbed, you take a nap, mother. I am giving you assurance you shall be completely cured very quickly."

Amrapalli was not satisfied with this answer and said: "But this is not your true recognition Jeebaka. Who are you?"

Jeebaka gave a wry smile on his face and answered: "The identity of a beggar is that of a beggar, mother. He does not have a father, a mother, a wife, a son, a daughter and a world of his own. He is only a beggar."

Amrapalli answered in an affectionate voice: "But you please sit near me for a moment, Jeebabka. Oh! My eyes are paining severely. Rub your hand on my forehead one more, Jeebaka."

Jeebaka rubbed his hand on her forehead like an obedient child. Amrapalli felt as if the inside of her being was cooled with a deep satisfaction and repose. Jeebaka, while rubbing his hand on her forehead, told: "This is the ultimate truth of this world, mother."

Amrapalli asked: "What truth, Jeebaka?"

Jeebaka answered: "This disease, this old age, this suffering! Youth is transient, mother."

Amrapalli asked: "Then what?"

Jeebaka answered: "In worldly enjoyment, there is no respite from that mess, mother. Sacrifice is the only path of liberation. That is why the prince Sakya Singh[23] is today a monk, the denouncer of the world.

Amrapalli asked: "Who is that Sakya Singh?"

Jeebaka said: "I shall his story today."

****

Amrapalli was slowly getting cured by Jeebaka's treatment and care. Her vision had not yet completely returned; yet, she was able to see everything, though a little unclearly.

---

23   The prince of the kingdom of Kapilabastu who later on renounced the world and became Lord Buddha.

That day when she saw Jeebaka for the first time, her heart was as if torn with the arrows of a hunter. This jeebaka—a beggar! If that abandoned child of her would have lived, he would have looked exactly like this man. The same appearance, the same vast forehead, the same eyes, the same sword-like nose! No! No! Why should Jeebaka be this filthy Amrapalli's bastard child? He is a god. What sense of un-fulfilment! What hunger! What desire! What desperation to clutch Jeebaka in her lap! Two streams of tears flowed form Amrapalli's eyes. Jeebaka asked: "Are you crying mother?"

"No! No! Why are you calling me mother? Call me Amrapalli; call me by whatever name you like." Amrapalli answered. But were these possibilities not in Amrapalli's life? If her own son would have been there beside her sick bed, if he saw tears in her eyes, he would have certainly asked: "Are you crying mother?" But here was Jeebaka who has sacrificed everything for the 'Sangha[24],' who had relinquished every pleasure of life for the sake of salvation."

Jeebaka asked again: "Are you crying mother?"

Amrapalli wiped her tear in her saree and said: "No Jeebaka! There is a pain in my eyes. You don't worry. The pain shall subside. Yes Jeebaka! You told me that day that you would tell me the story of Sakya Singh. Tell me the story now."

Jeebaka started telling Sakya Singh's story.

7

Gautama Buddha shall come to Baisali.

The news had spread in every corner of the city.

---

24   The Buddhist religious community.

The Lichhabis were busy in welcoming Gautama as per their customs. Baisali's men and women were desperate to see him, to get his blessings.

In the mean time, Amrapalli had been completely cured. She had gotten back her youth just like a moon being freed from Rahu[25]'s clutches. But the shades of dark clouds had closed upon her clear eyes and some unspeakable grief had taken out their lustre.

Jeebaka told: "Do you know mother? Lord Buddha is coming to Baisali."

Amrapalli said; "But how useful is that news to me Jeebaka? I am a whore. My body is an object for sale. Am I capable enough to have a look at the holy Buddha?"

Jeebaka answered with a smile: "Who is not a whore mother? Your body might be an object for sale. Not your life. But those who have made both their body and soul sellable are indeed worse and more despicable then you. These Lichhabis of Baisali! Have they not sold themselves in the name of the community? Have they not sold their conscience in the name of religion?"

In both the eyes of Amrapalli danced the flames of summer.

Today, King Bimbisara shall arrive. The messenger from Magadha had brought this news. Today Buddha will come to Baisali.

There was a huge commotion in Amrapalli's palace. Every corner was decorated with flowers. Amrapalli told Sirima: "Today, the guest will come, Sirima, the long-awaited guest."

---

25   It is, according to Hindu mythology, a devilish power that engulfs the moon in the dark moon night.

The full moon evening of spring! Amrapalli's mango orchard at Baisali's outskirts was filled with the fragrance of mango buds. After many days, Baisali was decorating herself in a world-beating, sensuous and beautiful attire. Chandra was helping Amrapalli wear the anklets, the golden thread in her dark, slender waist, and the golden bracelet in her arms. Sirimia was spraying her hair with the perfumes. Holding a mirror in her hand, Amrapalli was putting the vermillion in her forehead.

Everywhere there was a commotion; today will come the king Bimbisara. Like a river in the hill, Amrapalli's heart was dancing for today will come the Buddha, her long-awaited guest.

Amrapalli told in an excited voice: "Chandra, Shyama, Chhanda and Sirima! Don't delay any more, friends. The fool moon night's moon is coming up."

Sirima was decorating Amrapalli's wig with Ashoka[26] flowers.

The highway was filled with noises. Amrapalli ran towards the window and looked at   the noisy crowd. Somebody came and gave the news: "King Bimbisara is waiting for you in the luxury room."

Lord Buddha was coming. There was a huge and mad commotion amongst Baisali's citizens. Amrapalli came running from the window and told: "Hey! Here comes the guest Sirima! Let this luxury items be left here."

Amrapalli ran outside like a mad woman. From her dishevelled hair were falling many Ashoka flowers.

---

26   - A beautiful flower that blooms on the plant of *Saraca asoca* in the Indian subcontinent.

The poet's violin stopped. King Bimbisara rubbed his eyes with surprise.

The royal whores of Lichhabi community were speechless.

Gautama Buddha had accepted the invitation of spending time in Amrapalli's Luxury room. Amrapalli ran in her gorgeous attire and fell at the meditating Buddha's feet.

Buddha's disciples sang in a chorus:

> "Buddham saranam gacchami,
>
> Dhammam saranam gacchami
>
> Sangham saranam gacchami"
>
> (I take shelter in Lord Buddha,
> I take shelter in the holy religion,
> I take shelter in the holy community)."

****

The Smiling Krishna

It looked that day as if the sun halted his chariot for a moment to witness the last scene of *Mahabharata* in Indraprastha.

After the end of *Mahabharata*, Krukhsetra's abandoned battlefield was filled with the debris of many ornament-decorated chariots and with the heavily armed bodies of millions of Kaurava soldiers scattered all around. Their distressed wives led by late Duryodhana's wife Bhanumati madly ran through the field looking for their loved ones from amongst the mound of bodies. Their heartrending screams were sometimes submerging the terrifying shouts of dogs, jackals and the vultures.

Death had engulfed every commotion in Krukhsetra. Every sound including that of the horses and the tuskers had become silent under its terrifying spell. The battlefield was infested with swarming jackals whereas above in the sky were reeling like dark shades the flesh-loving kites in large flocks.

Dhrutarastra's palace in Indraprastha was quiet and people-less. At times Sanjaya and Bidura were found to be loitering inside the tranquil room with plaintive moods. The slow sound of their footsteps was making the climate grave and gloomy. Dhrutarastra's pitiful sighs and Gandhari's cries were getting heavier.

Dhrutarastra was blind from the birth. He had lost all his hundred sons, his friends and lieutenants including Karna, Drona, Bhurisraba etc. in Kurukhsetra's battlefield. His desire to see them for the last time ricocheted from the four walls of his room and then was silenced. But Gandhari thought of throwing away her eye-cover and seeing her son's bodies for the first and the last time; but her irrevocable vow during her marriage to Dhrutarastra, as a devoted wife, made it impossible for her. If she had not vowed that day, today she would have easily thrown away her eye-covers to see those bodies.

Gandhari was the mother of hundred sons — Duryodhana, Duhsasana,Durjaya, Duranta, Durgama, Durtara, Durbalaka; she was the glory of Somabansa[27]. The sons who slept only on the beautiful and comfortable cushions on their cots, now slept on their deathbeds in Kurukhsethra's muddy battlefield.

The rampage of dogs, jackals and kites on their bodies created a ghastly scene in the battlefield.

Gandhari emitted a sharp cry of pain at the intimidating sound of a flock of kites.

She lifted both her arms into the air and cried: "Bidura, Sanjaya . . ."

Her pitiful cry echoed for some time inside the hall and then was engulfed by the ghostly silence of the abandoned Kaurava palace.

****

---

27   The glorious clan into which Gandhari and the Kauravas belonged.

Blind Dhrutarastra lifted his two arms into the air with a futile arrogance and boasted before Bidura: "Don't forget Bidura! Even today I have the power to smash the killers of Kouravas—these Pandavas—in my two arms."

Dhrutarastra shouted like a lion on the Kaurava throne. The muscles on his wrinkled face stiffened. His eyes sparkled like a dead volcano come alive.

Bidura told in a cool voice: "Your Excellency, great king! All the Dhrutarastras are eternally blind. The power of the throne has blinded them forever. Eyes are not the only vision, king. Where was your vision when the Kauravas wanted to finish off the Pandavas in the lac- house? Where was your vision when the five sons of Draupadi were slaughtered in sleep? Where was your vision when Draupadi was denuded in the Kaurava palace before everybody? Where was your vision when Duryodhana boasted before Srikrishna's convoy that he would not give the Pandavas even a pinch of soil without war? If you had been just and right as a king during those times, today you would not have seen such dire consequences. That is why I keep telling that it is not just you, but it is all the Dhrutarastras who are perennially blind."

Dhrutarastra answered; "But I had never thought that the great warriors like Bhisma, Karna and Drona etc. will be defeated by the Pandavas."

Bidura answered: "That is why I keep telling that all the Dhrutarastras are perennially blind. The demands for justice by the exploited, however weak they may be, can never be suppressed by your huge and powerful Kaurava army. History shall always derogate and ridicule many Indraprasthas, many Hastinapuras and many Barunabantas for their meaningless arrogance. The great King! The peace and sovereignty of 'Bharata'[28] shall not be in the humiliation of the destitute, rather in uplifting them with kindness and fellow feeling."

Listening to Bidura's words, Dhrutarastra started shouting in a way as if the sky would fall. Lambasting Bidura with a grave voice, Dhrutarastra said: "Bidura! You are the slave of the Kauravas. You have grown up on the food and kindness provided to you by the so called arrogant Kauravas. Today, when they are in great distress, you are giving them the right gift with your unkind words. There is not even a word of comfort in your voice for the Kauravas."

Bidura responded with an unperturbed voice: "Great King! Truth however tough it may be has to be confronted one day."

Dhrutarastra shouted again: "But for a small state, the whole Kaurava race will be demolished. Do you agree to it, Bidura?" How would I forget Bidura? The lighted candles of the Somabansa are getting extinguished one by one. Like my own blindness, the future of my race looks blind, futile and gloomy."

Bidura responded in a cool voice; "The great king! Accept this fate as a result of your deeds. You will get peace. You have destroyed your own race by turning blind eyes to their misdeeds. Pandavas are only a small race. Don't harm them any more out of your anger and vengeance."

During that time, the grieving Gandhari came running like a mad woman with her eyes blindfolded and said: "Great king! One day I had wilfully put these covers on my eyes. Liberate me from my oath today great king. I am the mother of your hundred sons. I have never seen

---

28   The ancient name of India.

them in my eyes when I was living. Let me see them today when they are dead. Let my grieving eyes get some peace."

Gandhari wanted to tear off her eye-cover. In the process, her fingernails scratched her face and she started bleeding profusely. The blood oozing from her injured face made her look terrible.

Gandhari shouted again in an awfully broken voice: "Great king! I have always remained blindfolded because of you despite having my eyes that can see. Today, take off my eye-covers for once great king."

Listening to Gandhari's requests, Dhrutarastra's face became pale like a piece of dark cloud. Gandhari did not know (But Dhutarastra knew) that below the cover were not just Gandhari's eyes, but were two sleeping volcanoes. Once she opened them, even Dhrutarastra would burn to ashes.

Bidura tried to comfort Gandhari and told: "Try to control your grief great lady. Who tells you do not have sons anymore? Under the protection of the Pandava king Yudhisthira, your son Durdakshya is still alive." Moreover, the five Pandavas love and adore you like their own mother."

Gandhari started shouting again: "I know great king! This eye-cover shall never come out. Right from the beginning till the end, Gandhari's life is only about darkness and nothing else."

Gandhari came floating towards Dhrutarastra like a dry leaf; and then, went back in the same manner.

****

The chariot was ready. Yudhisthira was getting ready

to go somewhere alone. Right at that moment, Srikrishna approached him from an opposite direction and asked him: "On the eve of your coronation as the king of Hastinapura, where are you going alone Dharmaraja[29]?

Yudhisthira said; "Mother Gandhari wants to see me. I am going to meet her."

Srikrishna told: "I have also not met Gandhari for quite some time now. Then let's go together. I shall drive your chariot."

Yudhisthira was surprised by Srikrishna's words and asked: "What is this new mystery, Mayadhara[30]?"

Srikrishna sat on the charioteer's seat and said in a smiling voice: "I am the person who had led your victory-chariot in the great battle of Mahabharata. Are you doubting me, Yudhisthira?"

Yudhisthira kept quiet.

Srikrishna is always mysterious like this.

****

Gandhiri was roaming with Sanjaya through the mass grave of Kurukshetra's battlefront while looking for the bodies of her hundred sons. In the diminishing lights of the dusk, Sanjaya led her through the crowd of dogs, jackals and kites into the midst of these bodies scattered all around like dried leaves.

Sanjaya told: "Great lady! Look how the great man

---

29 Yudhisthira was famously called 'Dharmaraja' for being the protector of 'dharma' or righteousness.

30 Krishna was called 'Mayadhara' for being an expert in the art of creating 'maya' or illusion.

Bhisma lies out there on the soil in the deepest sleep of his life. Look at the deep, calm repose on his face."

Gandhari said: "I know Sanjaya! He has relinquished his life in his own will. Otherwise the Pandavas were nothing before his world-beating might."

Sanjaya said: "And here lies the war-hero Somadatta, smashed under the chariot-wheel and there lies the great Bhurishraba wounded to death by the mad tusker's tusks. Great lady! Here lies the war-hero Karna, hit by the arrows of archer Arjuna. On the broken crown on his head is stuck the last ray of the setting sun, like the blessing of the father on his son's head. With that ray, Karna's face still glows with the resplendence of a hundred blooming lotuses."

Gandhari held Karna's body in her breasts in a tight, passionate embrace and said in a choked voice: "Come boy! You have been deprived of a mother's affection all your life—

you, the greatest Pandava. Come to me. Let me embrace you. You, the protector of Duryodhana's arrogance! I cannot see you lying here on this muddy battlefield. But O almighty! O omnipotent! O creator! Is there no punishment for those who have defied the Khsatriya[31] principles and killed Karna in treachery?"

After moving some distance, Sanjaya told: "Great lady! Here is Duhsasana fallen on the soil, his thighs smashed by Bhima's mace. It was Bhima's vow to avenge his obscene behaviour towards Draupadi's denuded thighs in the Kaurava court. His pearl-decorated necklace still

---

31   It refers to the race of warriors. They are expected to fight the battles on the basis of certain heroic principles, not through deception.

dazzles on his wide chest, like the sparkle of lightening on blue clouds. Let's go great lady! This is the eternal game of life and death. Everybody is entitled to his deeds."

An outburst of a sharp cry of pain filled Gandari's voice and she told: "Remove my eye-cover once Sanjaya. This is the son whom I have never seen in my life. At least let me see his body and pacify my eyes."

A little away from Gandhari, Srikrishna slowed the speed of his chariot. Yudhisthira asked in an anxious voice: "Why did you slow the chariot's speed, Narayana[32]?"

Srikrishna answered with a gentle smile: "We should not go with the arrogance of victory to someone who suffers from pain and agony. In addition, Gandhari is like your mother."

Yudhisthira got down from the chariot like a wrongdoer and said: "You are absolutely right Narayana. I should go to grief-stricken mother Gandhari on foot."

Yudhisthira was slowly walking towards Gandhari sitting and bewailing near Duryodhana's body when Srikrishna pulled him back by one arm and said: "Do you know Yudhisthira why Gandhari has called you?"

Yudhisthira said: No! I do not know that."

Srikrishna smiled gently again and said: "Gandhari wants you to remove her eye-cover so that she can see the bodies of her sons from amongst the pile of bodies in Kurukshetra's crematory ground."

Yudhisthira told: "Is it a very difficult thing to do?" I shall tear off her eye-cover this moment."

Srikrishna smiled again and told: "But Yudhisthira!

---

32   Another name for Srikrishna.

How do you forget that the mother of hundred sons Gandhari is today sonless because of you?" In her understanding the whole of the Kaurava race has been demolished because of your aspirations for the throne."

Yudhisthira told in a helpless voice: "I don't know whether she knows it or not; but, you know it all great God."

Srikrishna answered: "After you uncover Gandhari's eye-cover, she would see her son Duryodhana's body first and then will she not be filled with a feeling of anger and revenge instead of that of love and compassion?"

Yudhisthira asked in a stupefied voice: "That is true Krishna. But when mother Gandhari has called me to do the job, what should I do?"

Srikrishna told: "All the hundred sons of Gandhari might have died; but her son Durdarsa is still alive. Gandhari's anger can be pacified when she sees her son Durdarsa."

Gandhari could hear Yudhisthira's voice from a distance when the former was conversing with Srikrishna and she asked Sanjaya: "Sanjaya! Is this not Yudhisthira's voice that I hear?"

Sanjaya said: "Srikrishna and all the Pandava brothers are coming to pay obeisance to you."

Excited, Gandhari lifted two of her arms in the air to embrace Yudhisthira and told: "Come, Yudhisthira, come! The living embodiment of compassion, the Pandava leader! Today you are also the Kaurava leader! I am the sinner; I have received the consequences of my misdeeds in the past. Please remove my opaque eye-cover once, son. I have never seen my hundred sons when they were alive; let me see them in their death for the last time and let me pacify my craving eyes.

Listening to Gandhari's pitiful words, Yudhisthira was going to remove her eye-cover; but Srikrishna stopped him from behind by holding one of his arms. Then he turned towards Gandhari's only surviving son Durdharsa and said: "Durdharsa! You go and remove your mother's eye-cover. The mother who has lost almost all her sons will at least get some comfort to see her one son living."

There was a mysterious smile in Srikrishna's lips.

Yudhisthira told Durdharsa: "Do what says Srikrishna."

At Yudhisthira's orders, Durdharsa immediately removed Gandhari's eye-cover.

The moment it was removed, the flames of anger and vengeance jumped from within the darkness of her eyes hidden beneath the cover. In those apocalyptic flames, Durdarsa turned into ashes within no time and fell on Duryodhana's body.

Yudhisthira shouted; "What did you do you cunning Srikrishna? Durdarsha was most loyal to me."

Srikrishna told in a slow voice "Keep quiet you moron. If you would have burnt into ashes in the flames of Gandhari's eyes, how would you have been coroneted tomorrow as Hastinapura's king? This is politics . . . Such sacrifices of these loyal and obedient Durdarshas in the furnace of politics is a routine thing. You should not be shaken so much by such a small incident, Yudhisthira."

Sanjaya told in a pitiful voice, as if struck by a

lightening: "What did you do great lady? You destroyed in your own hand the last insignia of the Kaurava race, Durdharsa."

Srikrishna feigned compassion and said: "Mother! Who says you are sonless? Who are the Kauravas and who are the Pandavas? They are all your sons. Now accept the Pandavas as your sons."

Another mysterious smile floated on his face.

Gandhari looked down at the mango-bud-like fallen body of Durdarsha at her feet and laughed loudly and said: "I have understood everything you crook! I have understood your plans. But mark my words Srikrishna! You can never retain the throne on the basis of your Sudarshan wheel's power. Everything shall be burnt in a grieving mother's curses. Even you won't be spared Srikrishna. Like the Somabansa, the Yadubansa[33] shall one day die out in internal conflicts. Even your favourite son Pradyumna won't be spared. This is my curse, the curse of a mother who has lost her hundred sons in the battle. My curse won't go in vain. Remember that Srikrishna. Remember that."

Crying uncontrollably, Gandhari also fell on the ashes of Durdarsa.

There was another mysterious smile on Srikrishna's face which however was weakening inside the approaching darkness.

In the western sky above the Indraprastha mountain range, the omnipresent sun was also shortly going to set in the west.

---

33   Lord Srikrishna's clan.

The Yadavas[34]

Tomorrow is Kumarapurnima[35]. The whole of Dwaraka is revelling. As a prelude to the main celebration, the Yadavas have started celebrating on its streets. Under the intoxicating spells of wine, they have crossed all limits of decency and self-control. The madness of celebration has spread all through the city's nooks and corners.

Near the window of his palace, Srikrishna breathed out a long sigh of helplessness that diffused into the gloomy air within no time. He had not perhaps taught these Yadavas the mantra of self-control. For a moment, he felt as if History is mocking him on his face.

Oh God! Akrura was saved by a fluke. Otherwise, he would have been smashed to dust under the wheels of Satyaki's madly speeding chariot. A baby was just now smashed under Pradyumna's chariot-wheels. Nobody paid heed to that. Everybody is madly engrossed in the celebration. Satyaki and Pradyumna were engaged in a charioting completion. The former laughed boisterously while passing ahead of the latter's chariot while the other

---

34   The Yadava dynasty to which Srikrishna belonged.
35   A Hindu religious festival.

Yadavas were thoroughly enjoying the competition. They started shouting loudly when Pradyumana now managed to go past Satyaki's chariot. The sharp cry of the dead baby's mother was lost in that congregated laughter.

Srikrishna kept watching helplessly the self-destructive madness of the Yadavas.

Akrura breathed out a long sigh and paused for a moment. But how would he console the mother who has lost her baby?

The mother was crying: "Hey Krishna! Hey Yadava leader! Hey Dwaraka king! How do you watch such madness of the Yadavas with open eyes?" But who would answer her? The Lord himself is dumb and helpless today. His own plight is pitiful.

But the Lord is mysterious. His mystery is inexplicable. But how could he silently witness such horrifying degradation of the Yadavas? How could he watch every step of the Yadavas towards self-destruction?

Akrura pondered deeply over this question and found no answer. There was no end to his inquisitiveness; but it was all in vain.

He thought of asking the lord today: "What is this new mystery, Lord?"

But he could not muster the courage to ask the Lord as his plight was deplorable. He was engrossed in deep and troubling thoughts. His usually bright forehead was today filled with frowns. His dazzling body looked terribly lacklustre. His lotus-eyes looked pale and lifeless. His face was full of a feeling of terrible sadness and utter displeasure.

What a pathetic and pitiable condition of the Lord of

the universe it was! The living epitome of joy and happiness was today deeply saddened and depressed. Akrura had never seen the Lord in such a condition. The Lord who had always remained cool and unperturbed even in the midst of the enemies in the *Mahabharata*, the Lord who had imparted Arjuna the ultimate wisdom of life, the Lord who had perennially remained cool, calm and composed in any adversity, how could he be so perturbed and distressed today? These thoughts greatly troubled Akrura's mind.

Akrura was slowly mustering some courage to ask the Lord this question. He would never leave him until all his questions were answered. He would fall at the Lord's feet, prostrate before him and not leave him until the latter did not clarify his doubts.

But Akrura still apprehended to enter into Srikrishna's dark and gloomy secluded chamber. But when he managed to slowly enter into the room, he was flabbergasted at the sight the Lord. It was no more the Lord's delightful, soothing face, but his violent, destructive image that Akrura was witnessing today. This image was once seen by Uttanka; it was seen by Duryodhana and Arjuna in the battlefield of *Mahabharata*. Akrura pleaded: "O Lord! Relinquish this destructive image of yours. I do not have the courage to see it even once. I want to see you in your calm and reassuring image. I want to see you as a fellow Yadava, as a fellow Yadava shepherd. I never want to see you in this terrifying, cataclysmic figure."

For a moment, Akrura was lost in a trance and then he suddenly came to his senses. Was it truth or an illusion? In a moment, the Lord reappeared before him in his reassuring human appearance. A wry, gentle smile splashed on his lips like a dazzling moon appearing for a moment in the cloud-infested sky. Akrura was reassured and then he asked the Lord in an inquisitive voice: "I am reassured my Lord. But what is this deplorable plight of yours? I am not able to bear it my Lord." Then Akrura prostrated before Srikrishna and asked in an almost asphyxiated voice: "Lord! Why are you playing this mystery with this deplorable slave of yours? Why is this inexplicable gloominess on your usually delightful face? Your plight pains me a lot my Lord. It pains me a lot. I cannot bear it."

Srikrishna's calm and soothing face suddenly became rough and cruel. The softness of his countenance suddenly disappeared. He said in an abrupt, cruel voice: "Leave Dwaraka this moment Akrura. Leave now. It's my order."

Akrura could not comprehend the meaning behind such sudden and cruel gesture on the Lord's part.

A cold shiver ran through his spine. Deeply saddened, he cried like an inconsolable baby and said and an almost asphyxiated voice: "What sin did I commit my Lord? I am no more than a dust particle under your feet. How can I leave Dwaraka without you?"

There was a faint glimmer of a smile in Srikrishna's lips.

At Akrura's plight, the Lord's voice turned soft and kind for a moment. He answered in a mellowed voice: "I had told Arjuna in Kurukhsetra's battlefront that there is neither sin nor piety in creation. All virtues and vices of a human being are part of Nature. Nothing is absolute in this world. There is no body in this world who can be fully virtuous or fully vicious. The man who possesses both virtues ad vices is dear to me. That is my concept of an ideal man. You be that ideal man, Akrura. Then you can also become dear to me."

Akrura was thoroughly perplexed by such ambiguity in Srikrishna's tone and asked in a stupefied voice: "Why this piece of advice to me, my Lord? I am not able to comprehend the mystery behind your words. What new mystery is this, my Lord?"

By now, the Lord's voice had completely softened and pacified. But it had now suddenly turned stoic. There was neither harshness nor indifference in that voice.

Akrura was still perplexed by this newfound stoicism on the Lord's face. His voice was turning more stupefied and anxiety-ridden. Akrura again fell on the Lord's feet and said: "Please stop this inconceivable mystery with me my Lord. I am not able to bear it."

With a gentle smile on his face, the Lord answered: "Why do you forget Akrura that I told Arjuna that my mystery is indecipherable?"

Akrura now wittily replied looking straight into the Lord's eyes: "My Lord! But I know you had also told Arjuna that the person who completely dedicates himself to you, you rescue him from the quagmire of your mystery. I am completely devoted to you my Lord. I am your slave, your disciple, your devotee. Please rescue me."

The Lord's facial expressions turned cruel and uncanny again. He said: "That is why I am telling you Akrura. Leave Dwaraka right now. I am telling you this for your good. This Dwaraka will be decimated Akrura. I do not want you to be destroyed like an insect in that blazing inferno that this city is shortly going to turn into."

Akrura answered: "But my Lord! You are the creator and the destroyer. Can you not rescue your favourite

Dwaraka and the Yadavas under the shade of your Sudarshana wheel[36]?"

Srikrishna answered in a cool and composed voice: "Do not forget my words Akrura. We are all the slaves of *time*. *Time* is the most powerful of all. It will engulf us all."

Akrura then answered: "If that is the case my Lord, then how can a nobody like me will survive *time's* onslaught? Its ineluctable cataclysm?"

Srikrishna assured Akrura with a soothing voice: "No Akrura! You are innocent; you are pious; you are devotional. You will survive this cataclysm and inhabit this beautiful Earth."

Akrura said: "But this beautiful Earth is meant for the Yadava heroes also, my Lord."

Srikrishna calmly answered: "Drunkenness with wine and arrogance is not a sign of heroism, Akrura. After our victory in *The Mahabharata*, the Yadavas have become more powerful. All this has happened because of me and you know that well Akrura. But their power and glory have now turned into blatant arrogance. They have lost their sanity and reason under its intoxicating spell. They have lost all virtues due to this arrogance. They have become slaves of their dirty senses. They have no more remained heroes. They have turned into slaves—slaves of their senses. I call him a hero Akrura who has mastered his senses. I had taught this sermon to the Yadavas. But today they have been maddened by their power and glory. Why would they remember me now?"

---

36   The Wheel that Lord Srikrishna held in his hand. By his order, the wheel severed the heads of the demons and the sinners.

But in any case, how could Akrura leave Dwaraka alone, without the Lord?

Akrura was preparing to resist when the Lord ordered him again in a stern voice: "You go from here Akrura. Let me contemplate. Do not disturb my tranquillity anymore. Please allow me to stay immersed in my aloofness and tranquillity. Yes, before you leave, you tell my orderlies to open my gold stashes."

Akrura said in a surprised voice: "But these drunken Yadavas will plunder those gold stashes my Lord. They will plunder them."

The same mysterious smile kept on floating on the Lord's lips. He answered in a curious voice: "Fire needs fuel to burn Akrura. Fire needs fuel to burn. How would their fire of arrogance burn without the fuel of my gold stashes? How would they turn blind in arrogance?"

Akrura still could not comprehend the mystery behind Srikrishna's words. Dumbfounded, he started walking away as Srikrishna said from behind: "Spread this message along the streets of Dwaraka—A Kokua[37] has come to Dwaraka. He will eat up and destroy everybody in the city."

"Kokua!" Akrura had never heard of such a name. Was it a ghost or a monster or something else? He pondered.

Srikrishna answered: "But the Yadavas would know it well. It's a beast with dishevelled hair, dark skin, a sinewy, dirty body, a dangling tongue, a pair of sunken eyes and a few sharpened nails. It's Kokua. It's death."

Akrura asked: "But O omniscient! O omnipotent! Can you not destroy that beast by your eternal powers?"

---

37   -An imaginary beast that was supposed to kill the Yadavas.

Srikrishna answered in a grave voice: "Akrura! I have told you already that even I am the slave of *time*. I am also a slave of destiny. I cannot change its course."

Srikrishna's orders were ineluctable. Akrura could not have defied them. He departed with a heavy heart. But while leaving, he was pondering over the insolvable mysteries of the enigmatic Srikrishna.

The huge uproar of the revelling Yadavas was audible from the streets. It was not a pleasant sound that was heard; it was an unpleasant uproar. It's an irony that Srikrishna once taught these unruly Yadavas the virtues of self-control. In a disturbed mood, the Lord got up and stood near the window.

There was Ambarisha moving on a chariot with an abducted Yadava lady. Addicted to wine and women, Ambarisha had lost all decencies and restraints. The abducted girl was shouting in helplessness crying for help. The shameless abductor Ambarisha was laughing loudly holding her hand firmly in his own. The lady's hair was dishevelled; her dresses were torn; her breasts were uncovered. Trying to cover her breasts with one hand, she was shouting: "O Srikrishna! O Lord! You had once rescued Draupadi from humiliation in the Kaurava Court by providing her countless dresses. How can you see me denuded on the streets of Dwaraka? Save me dignity O Srikrishna. Save my dignity."

A wry and indifferent smile splashed on Srikrishna's lips for a moment and then disappeared like lighting disappearing in the midst of clouds. Whose dignity he will rescue? Of this distressed lady? The Yadava ladies are also drunken; they have wilfully lost their dignity to these drunken men. With open bodies, they invite these drunken louts to disrobe them, to enjoy them. They do not have the piety of Draupadi; they do not have her devotion; they do not have her sense of surrender to the Lord. Rather, they have surrendered themselves before the lascivious desire of these Yadava men. Whose dignity then Srikrishna will rescue? The Sudarshana wheel on his left hand was despairing to sever the head of the lecherous, drunken lout Ambarisha. But Srikrishna restrained it from doing so as the crying lady was also a part of the self-destructive Yadava race. There was no point severing Ambarisha's head. Srikrishna thought that let the Yadavas destroy each other. Sudarshana wheel shall sever the last surviving Yadava's head. But it was to happen at a much later stage.

Srikrishna kept on watching through the window the self-destructive Yadava carnival. He could see two drunken wrestlers kill each other in a lethal wrestling bout on the field. Breathing out a heavy sigh, he came from the window to his throne.

Placing his heavy forehead on his delicate palm, the Lord asked himself: "What shall be the final consequence of this Yadava race?" By his mysterious designs, he could finish off all the Kaurava enemies on *The Mahabharata's* battlefront. All the great Kaurava heroes including Bhishma, Drona, Karna, Duryodhana, Jayadratha . . . all of them are now no more than dust particles on Earth. After a few days, these Pandavas will move to heaven. Only the Yadavas will remain. But will they survive with this mad craving for power? Srikrishna had given word to Arjuna that he will take multiple births to rescue the distressed from the exploiters. But now the Yadavas are no more distressed. They have become the exploiters. That day his son Shamba offended and humiliated the innocent monks on the streets of Dwaraka. Will the Yadavas respect the monks anymore? Will they uphold the glorious heritage of *The Mahabharata*? Srikrishna was deeply engrossed in these thoughts.

What crude joke destiny was playing with the Yadavas!

These Yadavas were once exploited and tortured by the mighty Kansa. Srikrishna did not hesitate to kill his own uncle to rescue these distressed Yadavas from his torture. He had also killed Kansa's favourite wrestlers Chanura and Mustika to protect the Yadavas from their threat. Then he had imparted the knowledge of self-restraint and spirituality to these Yadavas for which they became an illustrious race on Earth endowed with the qualities of heroism, divinity and glory. Known as 'Bashneyas' and 'Andhakas,' they surpassed the 'kshatriyas'[38] in terms of their valour and glory. Even the pride of Duryodhana was nothing before their pride. But how could now Srikrishna rescue them as they have thoroughly deviated from the path of virtue and spirituality, from the path of 'dharma'?

This is the Srikrishna who had eliminated the mighty Kauravas from the face of Earth to establish 'dharma.' He also did not hesitate to eliminate his own Kaurava disciple Durdharsa (the last surviving Kaurava, Gandhari's son) through deception. But for a moment Srikrishna remembered Gandhari's curse that not even a trace of the Yadava race will remain. Srikrishna started trembling like a palm frond at remembering Gandhari's curse as he knew her words would never go in vain. There were tears in his eyes as what he saw in his front was nothing but complete annihilation, an approaching apocalypse.

Today was perhaps the Yadubansa's dooms day.

---

38   People belonging to a warrior race.

Srikrishna could not have resisted it. He kept striking his forehead vigorously with his hand in frantic desperation.

Like a flock of swans came into the room his eight wives: Rukmani, Satyabhama, Jambabati, Nagnajita, Mitrabanda, Sulakhsana and Sushila. Srikrishna's chamber was filled with their beauty and fragrance. Srikrishna smiled at them instantly. But there was no sense of delight in that smile; rather it was dry, indifferent and wearisome.

Rukmani stroked the Lord's hair with her gentle, delicate palm and asked: "What are these dangerous premonitions my Lord?"

Srikrishna answered: "You eight wives of mine are experts in reading premonitions."

But Satyabhama asked with a sullen face: "Why did you drive away your favourite disciple Akrura so ruthlessly from Dwaraka, my Lord? Was it appropriate?"

Srikrishna answered: "There cannot be an answer to every question, my dear lady."

Then Nagnajita asked: "Why Daruka is opening all of Dwaraka's gold stashes at your orders? The Yadavas are plundering them."

Srikrishna answered: "Don't you know there is 'Kumara Purnima' celebration in Dwaraka? How would the Yadavas gift each other then?"

At this, Rukmani blasted at Srikrishna and said: "Will they gift each other by plundering our jewelleries? Is this your justice my Lord?"

Srikrishna answered: "What is the difference between pearl and lac? I had taught the Yadavas to consider both as the same thing. And they are doing the same right now."

At this Jambabati said: "Nobody can beat you in words my Lord. But is not an undeniable fact that the Yadavas today have turned into plunderers?"

Srikrishna answered: "To plunder others' wealth is the religion of the plunderers. If the Yadavas are plundering your wealth today, then they are remaining true to their religion. Why do you bother my dear?"

The eight wives knew that Srikrishna has always been a mysterious talker like this. Nobody could beat him in argument. He will discover his own mysterious logic to disprove the opponent. Even the greatest logical person like Arjuna has not been able to beat him in arguments and has been entangled in the net of his logic. How could these eight queens beat him in words?

Rukmani said: "We all know my Lord that you are unbeatable in argument. But would you please explain to us in simple terms the rationale behind your strange behaviour now?"

Srikrishna answered: "I have told you Rukmani there is not always an answer to every question. You please leave me alone and allow me to stay immersed in my own thoughts. What I need now is aloofness and tranquillity."

Emitting heavy sighs, the queens left his chamber. But Srikrishna's strange behaviour had tormented them, had deeply saddened them all. Srikrishna gave a parting smile at his women. But he knew quite well that now even they can be subject to abduction and ravishment by the Yadavas. The same Arjuna would be there with his Gandiba[39]; but won't be able to use it as Srikrishna would have taken away his power already.

---

39   The name of Arjuna's bow.

Srikrishna was again engrossed in deep thoughts.

The eternally tolerant Earth was also crying for help due to the atrocities of these maddened Yadavas. But how could Srikrishna destroy his own creation in his own hands? He was greatly troubled by these thoughts. Arjuna's dilemma in Kurukshetra's battlefront had also engulfed him. How could he destroy his own people? If that day he advised Arjuna to fight his kith and kin for the sake of 'dharma,' why could he not train himself accordingly and do the same today? "No! I cannot destroy my favourite Yadavas in my own hand." Srikrishna thought.

He left his throne and started loitering inside the room and explained to himself: "I had told Arjuna on the battlefront that if the mind and the intelligence of the human being are destroyed, the human being will automatically be destroyed. I have destroyed the Yadavas' minds; I shall destroy their intelligence. Without intelligence, they will turn self-destructive. I shall only be the indifferent watcher of their destruction."

A slow laughter filled the chamber for a moment and then mingled in its gloom.

Srikrishna could hear the unruly footsteps of the Yadavas on the stair. With an artificial expression of contentment, he sat on his throne. His conjecture was absolutely right. The Yadavas were coming in herds in the fear of Kokua.

With a gentle smile on his lips, Srikrishna asked: "What is the news Daruka? Why are you here leaving the 'Kumara Purnima' celebrations? Why are you here Manmatha? You Madhumatta? Where is the happiness of the Kumara Purnima celebration on your faces? Why are you so worried, Subahu?"

Subahu uttered only one word in a trembling voice: "Kokua! Kokua!" He could not utter anything more.

"Kokua!" Smiled Srikrishna and said: "I have never heard of any such beast."

"But Akrura told us while leaving Dwaraka that Kokua is coming to kill us all, to destroy Dwaraka. Kokua is a beast with dishevelled hair, dark skin, a sinewy and dirty body, a dangling tongue, a pair of sunken eyes and a few sharpened nails!" Said Manmatha in a trembling voice.

But Srikrishna asked: "Have any of you ever seen that beast?"

Daruka answered: "The Kokua is roaming from house to house deep in the night. He was going to tear apart my chest the way you tore apart Hiranyakashyapa's[40] chest. The moment I got up to get my mace, it dissolved in the night. I could not clearly see his face."

Everybody described their horrific experience of having confronted the Kokua in the night's darkness. But strangely, nobody had seen that beast yet. But how could have they seen it? The beast was coming stealthily in the darkest hour of the night, like a burglar. That is why every house of Dwaraka was closed just after the evening."

Srikrishna feigned being terribly disturbed and said: "After the battle of *The Mahabharata*, you khsatriyas claim yourselves to be the best warriors on Earth. And then, you fear this unknown beast so much?"

---

40 -A monstrous king in Hindu mythology whom Lord Bishnu killed by tearing apart his chest.

Daruka answered in a fallen voice: "But this is Kokua!"

Madhumatta said: "My Lord! You are the saviour of the Yadava dynasty. Only your Sudarshana wheel can destroy the Kokua. How can we be destroyed when you are here in Dwaraka?"

Srikrishna answered: "I had also answered to Arjuna on this on Kurukhsetra's battlefront. Man is his own enemy, is his own friend and his own saviour. Have you all forgotten my words?"

"But as long as your Sudarshana is in your hand, whom should we fear my Lord?" Said one amongst the Yadavas.

Srikrishna answered in a gloomy voice: "After the *Mahabharata* battle, my Sudarshana is powerless. In the pogrom for 'dharma,' its power has diminished. Its only power remains for the last killing."

Feigning helplessness, Srikrishna said: "The little power that Sudarshana has is to kill the last Yadava."

"Sudarshana i now powerless." Cried the Yadavas together.

In a feigned tone of reassurance, Srikrishna told with a smiling face: "After the battle of *The Mahabharata*, you are the best worriers in the world. You have earned great reputation on Earth in the name of 'Basneyas' and 'Andhakas.' Only you can destroy the Kokua. Now go and let me contemplate."

The Yadavas were departing being contented with the assuring words of Srikrishna when the former said: "Today is the full moon night. You be prepared for the dark moon night when you might have to confront Kokua for the last time. But you need not fear for you are the Yadavas, the heroes."

The Yadavas responded in one voice: "Yes! Yes! Today we are the best khsatriyas in the world. Whom should we fear?"

Then the Yadavas departed. A small ray of smile flashed on Srikrishna's lips and then disappeared like a waning moon in the sky."

The shout of the revelling Yadavas on the streets of Dwaraka had now intensified. They were holding maces and bows in their hands and making valiant protestations of their unmatchable valour and heroism. Today is Kumara Purnima. The dark moon night is yet to come. Srikrishna has also assured them that they can kill Kokua.

On the sombre and gloomy space of the city of Dwaraka, slowly descended the darkness of the dark moon night. Srikrishna kept staring at the calm, lifeless candle inside his chamber and got engrossed in deep thoughts. Outside, the Yadavas kept shouting: "Kokua," "Kokua" and their shout was so loud that it submerged the shouts of the incessant barking of wild dogs and the jackals.

Somebody shouted: "Hey! There went the Kokua."

Another Yadava said: "Where? Where?"

The first one said: "I had caught him by his hair. But it slipped off my hand and he escaped."

Another Yadava shouted: "Mace! Mace! Where is my mace? The mace in which I had smashed the Kauravas to dust!"

Another one shouted: "Where is my bow? Where is

my quiver? Where are my arrows? Oh! I have left them at home."

Srikrishna started laughing loudly. He was assured now that the intelligence of the Yadavas was now completely destroyed. Now they were the slaves of their senses."

Somebody shouted in the dark: "Hey! Here escapes the Kokua! Catch it Subahu! Catch it."

From the crowd, Satyaki asked: "Where did it escape?"

Another voice answered in the dark: "Into the forest."

Satyaki shouted: "I will see who will rescue you the beast? I am the great warrior Satyaki."

The Yadavas started running into the dark forest to catch the Kokua."

"Here is the Kokua! Hit it." Somebody shouted and Shamba started hitting a Kadamba[41] tree in the dark thinking it to be the Kokua. In that hit, 'Kadambari[42]' started flowing from the tree like a stream.

Somebody from amongst the Yadavas shouted: "This is Kadambari. I had never tasted such sweet Kadambari in my life. But where is the Kokua?"

"Oh! It's very sweet." Said somebody else from amongst the crowd.

Another one said: "Drink this Kadambari juice to the lees. Leave the Kokua and drink the sweet Kadamabri juice."

---

41   A tree in the subcontinent whose botanical name is **Neolamarck-ia Cadamba**.

42   The juice of the Kadamba tree.

The Yadavas now had left the kokua and were madly drunk with the Kadambari juice. They did not have control over their senses anymore. In the blinding darkness of that night and bereft of senses, they saw each other as Kokuas. Srikrishna stood beneath one Kadamba tree and enjoyed the rare scene of the Yadavas destroying each other in a strange, ghastly, suicidal act. Could his Sudarshana wheel ever have destroyed the Yadavas so easily?

Satyaki was shouting in darkness: "The Kokua escaped right in front of Shamba's eyes. If I was there in his place, I would have hit it to death with my mace." There was a clandestine ridicule in his voice at Shamaba's inability to kill the Kokua.

Shamba retorted in a taunting voice: "I know about your heroism in the battle of *Mahabharata*, Satyaki."

Satyaki answered by twisting his moustache: "How can you forget my heroism in that battle, Shamba? I had alone penetrated through Dronacharya's circle when nobody else could dare to do it. I am the real war-hero of *The Mahabharata*. It is only because of Srikrishna's propaganda that Arjuna is being hailed as *Mahabharata's* greatest worrier."

Shamba answered: "Hey Satyaki! How can you forget that Bhurishraba held you by your hair? It's me who rescued you from his clutch. How can you forget that?"

Satyaki answered to Shamba's taunt through a vigorous blow of his sword. Satyaki's severed head fell at a distance.

Leaving Kokua, Pradyumna came running towards Satyaki to attack him. Satyaki fell on the ground being hit by Pradyumna's arrows.

Then started a full-fledged war amongst the Yadavas themselves. There were attacks and counter-attacks with mace, with arrows . . . The whole battlefront was filled with cries and shouts and screams.

After end of the deep, dark night, the faint light of the dawn was blooming in the sky. The top of the dark forest was slowly getting lighted with sunlight. Inside the forest and on the ground, lied scattered the bodies of the slain Yadavas which created the illusion of another Kurukshetra battlefield.

Srikrishna looked at the ghastly scenario and saw that his favourite son Pradyumna was sitting beneath a 'kadamba' tree and was wailing uncontrollably looking at the bodies of his fellow Yadavas.

Pradyumna was a great and powerful worrier. But why should he have survived from Yadubansa's destruction? Srikrishna ordered his Sudarshana: "Sudarshana! Go and finish your last job." In a moment, Sudarshana wheel severed Pradyumna's head and came back to Srikrishna's hand.

Srikrishna said: "No! I do not need you anymore, Sudarshana. All my tasks have been completed. Now I have to endure the consequences of my own deeds. You are no more needed for me."

Saying this, Srikrishna threw off the Sudarshana from his hand.

The golden top of the Dwaraka city was slowly getting lighted with the blooming sun's light. For the last time, Srikrishna looked at the bodies of his favourite sons— Shamba, Aniruddha, Pradyumna and others.

Then with a gloomy disposition, he started heading in an uncertain direction.

In his front, was the call of the green forest—calm and soothing like death itself.

****

The Last Dinosaur

(I)

The car sprinted over Rupa Bridge in a hurried manner.

Maharaja[43] Rai Brajeswar Rai lifted the glass screen of the shutter and looked outside through the window. In the eastern sky, a greyish light was coming out slowly. The morning approached like a tearful lady.

Brajeswar Rai's head seemed heavier to him due to an overdose of whisky last night.

Yes... Rupa Bridge. Below the bridge, the zigzag stream of river Rupa laid on the sand like an exhausted woman who had slept with her partner last night.

Brajeswar lighted the extinguished cigar. Nothing really had changed in the last ten years. The same recognizable landscape on the very familiar banks of River Rupa! The same old station of Rajkanchangarh right in front! Nothing had changed.

Ten years were nothing. Brajeswar took off his woollen sleeping gown and threw it on the bed.

---

43   King

Returning to Rajkanchangarh even after ten years on this wintry morning made Brajeswar's drunken head fresh and rejuvenated. The vehicle slowed down when it got into the station yard. From the platform a loud chorus of multiple voices arose; it was a slogan in the Maharaja's honour. Brajeswar listened with keen ears . . . "Victory to Maharaja Brajeswar Rai . . . Long live Maharaja Brajeswar Rai." Brajeswar's cruel iron-face got wrinkled a bit with a thin ray of smile.

The train stopped. Brajeswar looked at the platform through the window. After an exile for ten long years, he was today returning to Rajkanchangarh. The platform was heavily crowded to welcome him and no single space was lying vacant. Of course, a lot had changed in the mean time. Rajkanchangarh no more remained a kingdom; the kingship was gone; the rust of age on Brajeswar's iron body was eminently visible. . .

Brajeswar opened the door of the compartment.

Three servants quietly came inside. One of them dressed him in his regal attire; another held a water pot and a towel to him such that he would wash his face and then wipe it off; another one brought the morning tea in a tray. Outside the compartment the slogan by the public 'Long live Brajeswar Rai' went on. His belongings were getting unloaded from another compartment. Lots of guns, many boxes, cameras etc.! Brajeswar slowly descended from the coupe onto the platform. It looked as if the quiet morning sky started shaking in his glory-slogans. Brajeswar's face was almost invisible from within the piling, dew-laden marigold garlands.

He smoked form his pipe and asked someone: "How are you Mahapatra? Are these all Rajkanchangarh's people?"

Nilambara Mahapatra answered: "These are Rajkanchangarh's people, Your Excellency. When they learnt that you are coming, they came here since dawn; they have decorated the gates and have placed beautiful pots on the roadside and have been waiting for you since then.

****

Another ten-year-old memory floated before Brajeswar's eyes. It was the tale of a dark night of September, 1942. The British political agent Mitchell Sahib told him in a whiskey-drunken, drowsy voice: "Brajeswar Rai! You have to leave Rajkanchangarh right now by the orders of the mighty British government. It's an exile of five years for you."

Outside the Rajkanchangarh palace, the agitated mob stood lined for the blood of the tyrant Brajeswar with country-made rifles and dynamites in their hands. This Nilambara Mahapatra was the person who had that day clandestinely led Brajeswar to safety and left him in the railway station. Nilambara Mahaptra was the trusted lieutenant of this cruel, inhuman Brajeswar Rai. After that, he also spent three years in the jail in charge of many misdeeds.

Mahaptra shouted at the mob: "Give way you rascals. Give way to the king."

A Roles Royse car came and parked at the gate with great difficulty after pushing away the accumulating mob. Brajeswar got into the car. Nilambara Mahapatra sat in the driver's seat and drove the vehicle.

Though Brajeswar's appearance had undergone many changes over the years, the same regal cruelty persisted on his thin body and on his pale forehead filled with dishevelled hairs. The cruelty also sparkled through the penetrative vision of his razor-sharp eyes.

Brajeswar told; "Drive fast Mahapatra! I should reach the fort in an hour and fifteen minutes." The fort was seventy miles away from the station; but the vehicle was running at a speed of only ten miles per hour.

Mahapatra increased the vehicle's speed a little and told: "Sir! It's really difficult to drive fast through the mob."

They would have just met with an accident. A person was coming to garland the vehicle's bonnet.

Brajeswar shouted at the mob: "Fools! Don't you know that obstructing the public road is a punishable offence?" Then he instructed Mahapatra to drive faster.

But Mahaptra argued; "Sir! These rascals have come from long distances to honour you, Your Excellency."

Brajesawr left out a mouthful of smoke and said; "One day these rascals came from long distances and accumulated here to drink my blood. Neither their love nor their enmity has any value for me. I cannot act before them with folded hands. You drive fast, Mahapatra. You drive fast."

The vehicle vanished with loud horns in the midst of a rising whirlwind of reddish dust at its back.

(II)

In the garden of the Rajkanchangarh palace, Brajeswar was loitering with a gun in his hand.

In the blue sky, were flying flocks of cranes, kites and sparrows. Somewhere else, across the sky was flying another flock of till ducks, like a garland of jasmines. Brajeswar aimed at them and fired from his gun. Some birds fell at his bullets. A feeling of contentment bloomed on Brajeswar's iron-face. A gardener ran to search for the dead and the injured birds.

Another flock of birds was coming with loud twitters.

Their thirst for life was not quenched at the Caspian Sea. The chilling winter there propelled them towards the equatorial areas for the warmth they offered. In their wings there was a call of distances; in their throats, there was the song of life... Brajeswar aimed at them once again and fired. Some till ducks fell fluttering at the bullet wounds. From their multi-coloured wings, fell tiny drops of blood onto the ground.

Brajeswar lifted one bird in his hand. Death was slowly engulfing the bird. Brajeswar threw it on the ground without a feeling of remorse or mercy.

****

These days Brajeswar no more enjoyed such wastage of energy in killing birds. There was no excitement any more in killing. He slowly walked back towards the palace placing the gun on his shoulder.

The white shade of the palace danced on the crystal-clear water of the pond. Brajeswar was startled by the twitter of a bird from within a tranquil cypress bush.

The palace looked still and quiet, bereft of anybody's presence. An atrocious, companionless and meaningless futility reigned over there! Everywhere a profusion lifelessness! Brajeswar slowly walked towards the palace with a buried head.

In the front portico, some people were waiting to greet him. At the news of his arrival at Rajkanchangarh after so many years, a lot of citizens of his lost kingdom were coming from distances to meet him every day. The kingdom was gone; the kingship was gone; yet, the love, the loyalty and the allegiance of the citizens for the king still lingered in their subconscious—firm and unshaken. Looking at Brajeswar, they fell at his feet and paid him regards. Brajeswar did not pay any heed. He took off his gun from his shoulder and handed it over to a servant and quietly went inside the palace.

Inside the palace, Brajeswar asked Mahapatra: "Why have these people assembled here? What do they need? Drive them away."

Mahapatra told: "Sir! The way time is changing, it's profitable to keep them in hand. Shall it be appropriate to drive these rascals when they have come with so much of love and adoration for you?"

Brajeswar answered in a slightly agitated voice: "Yes! Times have changed. But I have not. Neither do I have any desire to change."

Mahapatra left.

Everywhere there was the cruel, pitiless laughter of lifelessness! And also was everywhere the meaningless profusion of opulence... The multicoloured rose garden was clearly visible through the open window. It seemed as if life was nothing but the lifeless marble statue of a beautiful lady. She could be felt, but could not be enjoyed; she could be drunk; but that won't quench your thirst. Here was no dust, no dirt, no darkness; everything was bright here. And here is only a violent desire for flesh and brute force to satisfy that.

Brajeshawr called: "Who is there?"

Some insider came and stood for an order. Brajeswar ordered: "Whisky and Soda."

They were brought immediately. Brajeswar sipped some whiskey from the glass and placed it near him.

Mahapatra came and told: "Your Excellency! Damodar Raiguru has come to meet you".

Brajeswar asked: "Which Damodar Raiguru?"

Mahapatra told: "The same Damodar Raiguru of Ranidaha who had girdled the palace with armed rebels during the citizens' revolt. Let me send him back telling him that he cannot meet you."

Brajeswar said: "No! Send him straight to me, Mahapatra. Send him straight to me."

After some time came Damodar Raiguru. He was a fairly aged man. He was a participant of many revolutions and had gone to prison many a times. The torture he received in jail was still visible on his face as a clear imprint. Damodar paid regards to Brajeswar with a bent head.

Brajeswar asked: "What new demands do you have Raiguru? I have fulfilled all your demands."

Raiguru smiled and said: "What demand, Your Excellency? Nothing! Things are going from bad to worse here, in Rajkanchangarh."

Brajeswar told: "That is quite ok. You are destined either for the good or for the bad. God has written nothing more in your forehead."

Raiguru asked: "Means?"

Brajeswar lighted his pipe and said: "The meaning is very simple Raiguru. To exploit is the nature of man. Man created the nation to protect one weak person from getting exploited by a stronger one. But the nation became more atrocious and exploitative than the man himself. Tell me who had thought of it?"

Raiguru asked: "Then why did we put an end to monarchy?"

Brajeswar left a mouthful of smoke from his pipe and answered: "There was a huge flaw in monarchy, Raiguru. I was exploiting and torturing the citizens without their consent; but democracy does the same with their consent. For instance, in monarchy, I could crack your head without your permission; but in democracy, I can do the same with your permission." After uttering these words, Brajeswar started laughing loudly.

Raiguru said: "Even I have started believing in exploitation, Your Excellency. Man does not believe in anything else other than exploitation. The human civilization, society, culture, religion and knowledge— everything is built on the foundation of fear. As long as exploitation is there, the human society shall continue to remain safe and secure. If there is no fear of exploitation, then man cannot be bonded in the incarcerations of the society."

Brajeswar left into his room. He did not have time for such meaningless discussions.

III

It was evening time.

Brajeswar was standing near the window of his rest room and looking at the moon-blanched garden outside.

From within the foliage of the Eucalyptus and casuarinas trees, the full-blown moon was rising slowly like the image of an unknown prince rising in the dreamy eyes of the princess. Brajeswar had finished off all the whiskey from his glass. Coming back from the window, he sat on a sofa. The severed heads of some tigers hunted at different points of time hung on his wall like taxidermy—an unsatisfied hunger brimmed on their huge, burning and terrifying tongues. The hunger was still alive in them even after their death. A ghostlike silence reigned supreme in the room. Inside, the dim electric bulb emitted almost unrecognizably thin rays.

Brajeswar pressed the electric switch of the calling bell near him. Within some time, Nilambara Mahapatra came in. Brajeswar lighted his pipe and said: "The evening is beautiful, Mahapatra."

Mahapatra said: "Yes, Your Excellency! The evening is really beautiful."

Brajeswar left a mouthful of smoke from his pipe and told: "But Mahapatra! The beauty is not to be enjoyed alone. Have you arranged for something? I mean a virgin— untouched, uninitiated . . ."

Mahapatra answered with the tone of an apologist: "Sir, gone are those days when we could drag anybody to your feet. The time has grown difficult."

Brajeswar said: "What is the problem? First there was the fear of the ruler; we had the power to confiscate something from somebody by the sheer display of fear. But now can we not do the same with the power of money?"

Mahapatra answered with a clear and unambiguous gesture of disapproval: "I don't believe so, Your Excellency. It cannot be done now."

Brajeswar took another peg of whiskey and drank it silently. Then he lifted the emptied glass before his eyes for a few seconds and told while surveying something inside it: "I have heard Mahapatra, you have a rare diamond inside your own house. Why should you look for it outside?"

Nilambara Mahapatra's eyes lit up like two burning pieces of coal. His expressions became harder. He said in an enraged voice: "I am indebted to you for life, Your Excellency. But I have not eaten up my conscience. No father in this world can accept such dirty proposal. I cannot believe my ears."

Nilambara Mahapatra was leaving the room. Brajeswar called form behind: "Listen Mahapatra."

Nilambar stopped like a statue at Brajeswar's orders. Brajeswar walked a few silent steps inside the room and told: "You have violated your conscience many a times in the past to keep your allegiance to me, Mahapatra. And you know that quite well. Do you remember how many hundreds of times you have ordered fathers to send their daughters to me?"

Nilambar said: "Forgive me, Your Excellency. I cannot do it anymore. It's my own daughter."

Brajeswar threw a bunch of keys at Brajeswar and said: "Open that iron safe."

Nilambara Mahapatra opened the iron safe like a robot. It was full of gold jewelleries. His eyes lit up at their blinding resplendence.

Brajeswar said: "The royal mother had kept all these jewelleries for the future queen of this royalty. You know Mahapatra! I love to confiscate things rather than obtaining them as gifts. And you know that quite well. But rest assured that no single lady has wore these ornaments even once. If you wish, your daughter can wear all these."

Nilambara looked at Brajeswar like a hypnotized man. Brajeswar told: "I shall decorate her in my own hands as per her wishes."

Nilambara sat on a couch for a moment like a dumb statue.

Brajeswar told: "I am waiting. You come quickly."

IV

It's was deep in the night.

Outside, the full moon night's moon was ready to set. The garden in front of the palace was slowly getting covered by a moving, liquid darkness.

Brajeswar poured the last few pegs of whiskey from the bottle into the glass and told: "Sundari! You have a beautiful name. There is no exaggeration in your name; it's easy and simple. You are truly beautiful."

Sundari was Nilambara's daughter. Brajeswar had heard it right. She was incomparably beautiful.

Sundari stood near Brajeswar with a half-buried head, like an injured deer hit by the hunter's arrow. She did not have the courage to look at his ruthless, drunken face.

Brajeswar told again: "Why don't you come closer, Sundari? Why do you stand there alone?"

Brajeswar lifted the veil from her head and held her chin in his hand. There was a dark mole in her chin.

Brajeswar told: "This mole on your chin looks beautiful like the secret love of a bride."

Sundari kept quiet like a dumb cow.

Brajeswar undressed her in both his hands. She stood naked before him, like the shy, moonlit night outside. Her breasts were uncovered. Her thighs were as if made of marbles by an adroit artisan by sheer hard work.

Brajeswar told: "It's a beautiful symmetry." Sundari blushed and covered her face with both of her hands.

Brajeswar removed the remaining dresses from Sundari's body in his own hands.

While resisting, Sundari's hand hit the dark mole on her chin. It got partly erased and ran like a line along her cheek. The mole was in fact drawn by her in collyreum to make her face look more attractive.

Brajeswar said: "Your mole is erased now, Sundari. What was the need for you to paint your rosy cheek with a brush?"

Sundari sat on the sofa with her face covered by her hands in mixed feelings of shame and fear, like a stone-carved effigy made by a sculptor.

Brajeswar walked silently inside his room with his arms folded against his chest.

He stood near Sundari and asked: "Can you tell Sundari which is more beautiful? The lecherous eye of a man or the nudity of a woman's body?

Sunadri looked at Brajeswar, dumbfounded.

Brajeswar opened the iron safe in his own hands and told: "These are all yours, Sundari. You take whatever you like. Your price! I am leaving. You can close the door from inside."

Brajeswar left the room and went outside. Undressed, Sundari was looking speechlessly at him. At the distance, his footsteps dissolved in the darkness of the night.

****

A Spring Night of Grief

It was already past 12 o' clock in the night. Hrudaya Babu was still not able to sleep even after taking two 'calmpose' sleeping tablets. No! These tablets were not working anymore; they had become ineffective. A little while ago, the sound of a drunkard's moving feet were faintly audible from the empty road. . . He was returning from an alcohol-club. His feet were moving unsteadily, sometimes to the left, sometimes to the right. That sound in the tranquil night echoed in Hrudaya Babu's ears and broke his tired sleep. At least something was happening in his companionless and uneventful life. There was a living human being in his vicinity and this feeling was giving him comfort. But slowly even that sound dissolved in the quiet night.

Outside, was spread the crimson moonlight of the spring night. Through the right side window, a splash of that moonlight had fallen scattered on Hrudaya Babu's wide, open chest and on the empty bed.

Time is very strange... One day this beautiful splash of moonlight scattered on the bed could ignite fire in Hrudaya Babu's excited nerves and tendons. Even today, it ignited his mind and spirit despite his sick body and approaching old age. The same moon light, the same spring night, the same hypnotic south-wind! That day, this moonlight became a beautiful ornament in the soft, sensuous body of Hrudaya Babu's bride. But now she has grown old and feeble, and has taken recourse to spirituality. She spends most of her time in 'Puja[44]' and other spiritual activities inside the worship room and when she comes to the bed, she starts chanting God's name till she sleeps. At times when Hrudaya Babu becomes a little naughty with her for a change, what shrilling and repelling sound she makes! She shouts: "Shameless fellow! Characterless fellow!" Thank God! She has gone to Puri for the last two days. She has gone to bathe in the sacred sea and to see the holy face of Lord Jagannatha. She will spend at least one week there. Hence, this week shall be a week of unbounded freedom, of enjoyable freakishness for Hrudaya Babu. But what shall he do with this meaningless freedom with this arthritis-affected body? He can only look at this fickle spring moonlight with open eyes while fallen on his bed and doing nothing else...

Yet this freedom, this liberty was alluring, attractive. Now he did not have to worry about his wife's admonitions to take the medicine in the right time; he no more feared the ghosts of diabetes and hypertension; he no more had to compulsively read *Geeta* or *Bhagabata* sitting on his wheel chair; he did not have to sit beside and bow to the strange rules laid down by a 'Baba' caught from somewhere by his wife. There was no shout, no allegations of being a shameless, characterless fellow by his wife when he sat with his whiskey bottle on the chair.

But this aloofness, this alienation was tormenting. There was some satisfying sense of companionship even

_____

44   Worship of any Hindu god or goddess.

in a quarrel with the wife. There was a sense of keenness even in this acute and deteriorating conjugality. After his wife Surama Devi went on the pilgrimage, a terrible sense of aloofness and alienation had completely engrossed Hrudaya Babu.

Today this moonlit night of the spring! This moonlight! This fickleness of this south-wind! And this lifelessness, this aloofness! And this paralysed body!

Hrudaya Babu took out a cigarette case from below his pillow and tried to light his cigarette. These days he found it difficult to light the cigarette by himself. The matchsticks were all getting extinguished the moment they were lighted by the fickle wind coming through the window. After trying hard for many times, Hrudaya Babu finally succeeded in lighting a cigarette and then, took a mouthful of smoke inside and then, left out some of it. The curl of the smoke was visible in the moonlight. Hrudaya Babu felt like conquering a hitherto unconquered mountain range.

Who shall believe today that once during his youth, Hrudaya Babu was a tireless hunter? Who can imagine that he roamed through the mountains with a rifle in his hands, day in and day out? Hrudaya Babu spent most of his life in the hills and jungles as a conservator of the forests.

In the tranquillity of the garden in the night, the sound of someone's footsteps was heard. No! It was perhaps the semblance of a sound in his illusion—he thought. A few street dogs on the road started barking. The Alsatian dog in the neighbourhood barked for a few times and stopped. Everything became silent again.

Hrudaya Babu returned to his past laden with sad

and happy memories. With this paralysed body, he could not imagine that one day he had a happy, exciting and exuberant youth.

Those days, his nights were spent in the empty, marooned bungalows. But even for once, he never felt the bites of his aloofness, of the emptiness of his surroundings. The beauty of the forest had mesmerized him; the golden deer's golden eyes had maddened his desire.

But Hrudaya Babu could not write a single poem in his life. He had many times tried to write; but even once, he did not like his own poems. He could never capture his heartfelt feelings correctly on pen and paper. Hrudaya Babu never liked his own poetry. He kept tearing off and throwing away his own poems.

But still, he has always remained a dreamy, romantic, and poetic mind.

Suddenly was visible outside the window the silhouette of a human head. Hrudaya Babu got up with a jerk. Initially he did not understand anything. He felt as if the man was cutting the wires of the grill with some cutting machine. Its sound was faintly audible.

Hrudaya Babu understood instantly that this man is either a thief or a dacoit. Then he felt there is no use calling the servant Mangulia as he usually slept so deep that he won't get up to his call. He required a fire brigade bell to get up from sleep. He must have smoked opium and fallen deep asleep somewhere. Hrudaya Babu tried to get his revolver from below his bed. But he immediately remembered that it was not loaded. Surama Devi found it difficult to sleep if he kept a loaded revolver below the bed. Then what was the use of keeping a revolver? But women don't understand the logic. By this time, the man had entered inside the house by cutting the window-grill.

Hrudaya Babu switched on the bed light. Seeing a human figure in the dim blue light, he got terribly scared. The man was wearing a short black pant; he had lots of hair on his wide, open chest and a quadrangular locket hung from his neck through a black thread. He had a huge and curly black moustache and had tied a handkerchief on his head. Hrudaya Babu thought that the man has recently joined the profession.

The man was also startled to see Hrudaya Babu right in front. Hrudaya Babu thought let him loot whatever he likes for he does not have the strength to stop him. But let him at least have the companionship of a man in the midst of this brooding, tormenting aloofness.

Hrudaya Babu told: "Hey man! Sit here. Why are you getting so desperate? I am giving you the keys of this steel cupboard. You do not need to take out your knife or something and threaten me. You are actually a friend of the rich people. But they call you a dacoit. You take comfortably whatever you want to take. But before that, come and sit with me and help me lighting my cigarette. Let's sit down and talk. Do you fear I will call the police? See! The telephone lies there, at a distance. Moreover, I am a disabled man. So, you need not worry. Please sit on that wheel chair. There is no other chair nearby.

That man found himself absolutely dumbfounded at Hrudaya Babu's kind and friendly words. Then he sat quietly, as per the former's instructions, on the wheel chair. He lighted his own cigarette and also lighted Hrudaya Babu's cigarette.

At a distance on the road, a moving car almost met with an accident. It would have dashed into the roadside sewage; but the driver put the break in the right time. But the sound of its wheels rubbing against the soil was largely audible through the deathlike tranquillity of the night.

The man suddenly got up from the chair and took out a knife from his pocket and brandished at Hrudaya Babu and said in an aggressive tone: "Keys . . ."

Hrudaya Babu said: "Keep that knife in your pocket friend. I told you don't need to brandish that at me. The keys are with my wife who is now in Puri. See below the pillow. There might be a duplicate key."

The man kept brandishing that knife at Hrudaya Babu in the right hand and inserted his left hand below the pillow and got the duplicate key. Then he opened the steel cupboard and went on scrambling the racks with both his hands. There was no other thing in the brief case except a few papers.

There was no sense of fear or apprehension on Hrudaya Babu's face. Rather he looked like enjoying the scene. The burglar was examining two fixed deposit forms in the light. Hrudaya Babu said; "Hey friend! You will get bundles of currency notes in the steel cupboards of ministers and leaders. They don't keep them in banks to evade income tax. But all our money is in the bank. Those two pieces of paper will not be of any use for you. Those are fixed deposit forms."

The burglar threw the two fixed deposit forms on the ground, and went on scrambling more in the shelves, in the brief case. From within the brief case, he found a gold necklace and two finger-rings.

Hrudaya Babu told: "Friend! If you don't take that necklace, I will be greatly obliged. It is my younger daughter Sujata's. She is no more. The day when she first went to college, I had bought this necklace for her. She used to go to college wearing it. Hrudaya Babu drew in a huge breath that looked like intensifying the fickleness of the night into intense grief. By that time, the man had splayed the whole floor with almost all of Surama Devi's costly sarees from the cupboard along with some of Hrudaya Babu's dresses. The gold necklace and the finger-rings had by that time slipped into the man's pant pocket.

In the dim blue light of the bed, there were shining in the cupboard shelf two whiskey and one vodka bottle. The man had taken out the vodka bottle, but Hrudaya Babu told: "Don't bring that vodka bottle, friend. I don't have tomato juice. There is also no soda. If they were there, I would have made excellent bloody-merry cocktail for you. Even today, I am known for making excellent cocktails, my friend. Rather you bring that whiskey bottle. It can be drunk with water. This is not your cheap, country-made liquor. This is sophisticated foreign scotch. It's the customs thing."

That man held the vat-69 bottle and sat on the sofa.

Hrudaya Babu told: "The adjacent room is the dining room. Please take a little trouble, my friend and bring two glasses along with one bottle of water."

The man obliged and sat on the sofa after bringing a bottle of soda and two glasses from the dining room.

He poured three pegs of whiskey all at once into the bottle. It looked as if that is how he drank his alcohol, to gulp large doses without even water. Perhaps that is why he was not accustomed to measured pegs. He did not require water at all and finished off the glass in a single breath, and then lighted a cigarette. Hrudaya Babu, on the other hand, poured a peg of whiskey in his glass.

Hrudaya Babu said: "The flavour of scotch is different my friend."

The man poured a lot more from the bottle into his glass. Perhaps only one peg remained at the bottom of the bottle.

But suddenly there was heard on the road the frequent whistles from the patrolling police van. The man apprehended a little at the whistles. According to newspaper reports, some 'khalistani[45]' terrorists had encroached into the city. That is why the frequency of police patrolling had increased of late. It would continue incessantly till dawn.

The man switched off the light.

Hrudaya Babu still kept on liking the man's company, even if he was a burglar. For a long time, he had not enjoyed a live man's company over a few pegs of whiskey in an unselfish conversation. He hardly had occasions for such intimate one-to-one conversations except with specialist doctors over his medical issues.

With a whiskey-filled glass in his hands, Hrudaya Babu's night-friend looked like having completely forgotten the former's presence in his vicinity. Perhaps he felt a little uneasy in Hrudaya Babu's presence.

The man did not know to talk in a relaxed manner— thought Hrudaya Babu. In one gulp, he was finishing off

---

45   The Sikh terrorists of Punjab who wanted a separate land form them known as khalistan.

pegs of whiskey. He had now started looking at the other bottle on the cupboard-shelf.

Hrudaya Babu told him: "Quickly change your black short pant, 'night-friend.' I know you will never reveal your name to me. That is why I have named you 'night-friend.' If you go outside now with this short pant and these pair of dark glasses and with this bull's figure, then you might face terrible dangers. People might think you are a dacoit. That's why please do what I say. Please change your dresses."

The 'night-friend' wilfully obliged. He kept the whiskey glass on the table and changed his dresses as quickly as possible.

Hrudaya Babu left another mouthful of smoke into the air and said: "That's better. You now look like a thorough gentleman. Ha! This figure! These so called gentle and savage figures! All are tailor-made. These tailors and these saloon-people are the ones who portray some men as gentlemen and some as savages. Now if someone sees you outside in this gentle dress, would anybody say that you dashed into my house as a looter by cutting the grills of my gate? Now you look either like a leftist leader or like an artist, 'night-friend.' Cheers..."

The 'night-friend' answered in a heavy, whiskey-drunk voice; "Ha! For your kind information, I am a postgraduate from a university. M. A. in Political Science..."

"But I am unemployed, jobless..."

Hrudaya Babu responded in a taunting voice: "Then you must have cleared your exam. through malpractice."

The 'night-friend' answered in an angry voice: "So what! That is the system of education today. You pass either through malpractice or through some connection. But my certificate is genuine."

The 'night-friend' continued: "I have appeared in many job interviews, but could not succeed in one. I remained unemployed for quite a long period of time. Then I once heard a minister's speech that our youth should find ways for self-employment. I got inspired by his speech and found out that this is the best method of self-employment — burglary. Now this is my career, my illustrious career."

After telling this much, the 'night-friend' took a long, deep breath inside.

Hrudaya Babu remained speechless for a moment.

The 'night-friend' went on: "But you disappointed me a lot, my friend."

Hrudaya Babu enquired: "How? How did I disappoint you after so much of hospitality?"

The 'night-friend' answered: "After specializing in grill-cutting, I came here to your house for the first time, to cut your grill. I had heard that you are paralyzed. Your wife is on pilgrimage. Your servant is an opium-addict. You were a forest-conservator. You have hidden a lot of wealth inside your house. But what I find here is nothing. Whatever little is there, it's all chickenfeed. You do not have a sandal-wood cot. You do not have any wealth. Or is it your shrewdness? Have you dug your wealth somewhere? Does a dacoit burgle into someone's house in the middle of the night to have a gentle talk with the owner over a few pegs of whiskey? To exchange pleasantries? Nonsense! My whole night is spoiled."

Hrudaya Babu answered: "You trust me friend.

Whatever I may be, I am not at all shrewd or cunning. I kept on hunting through the forest all my life. When the hunter and the prey confront, no shrewdness would work. Either you kill it or it will kill you. My whole life was spent running after the mysterious animals of the jungle. I was enchanted by the mystery of the forest my friend, by its mystery and its beauty. I spent all my time, all my life pursuing that. How could I then have made for myself cots of sandal-wood? Then also my friend! We were people of the old generations. We did not know this craft of stealing. We used to fill the forests with sandal-wood plantations. Now these wood-mafias are smuggling sandalwood, and the corrupt govt officials are buying them through their black money and are making sandalwood cots from them."

Outside, there was the sound of police patrolling vans. A motor cycle passed by making a loud noise.

Perhaps this was the police's last round of patrolling. Some early morning birds twittered on the trees of someone's garden and then became silent. The moon had waned in the sky. The sky was slowly getting filled with light, greyish patches. In a few moments, those greyish patches would slowly turn reddish with the nascent rays of the blooming sunlight. In the meanwhile, the 'night-friend' had almost finished his second whiskey bottle.

At a distance on the main road, the thunderous sound of a truck was largely audible. The 'night-friend' who had come in silently through the cut grill, was now trying to jump through the window with all his dresses and grill-cutting-tools in a bag.

Hrudaya Babu's eyes had slowly gotten heavier with sleepiness. He told the 'night-friend': "If you come another time friend when my wife is not here, I will prepare for you a bloody-merry cocktail in my own hands."

Hrudaya Babu managed to force away his drowsiness and got up to drink the last peg of whiskey that was left in the glass. The 'night-freind' had left and also had left on the bed the former's daughter Sujata's necklace and finger-ring.

Hrudaya Babu lifted the necklace and the finger-ring in his hand and suddenly became serious and sentimental. He caressed the gold necklace with his hand and emitted a long, deep breath from his lungs. It looked as if that infused some warmth into the cold breeze of the wintry dawn.

His two eyes were slowly getting closed with sleep.

****

The Floating Moon and
the Cold Bread

A labourers' demonsration continued in the capitalists' textile mills since the last month.

Despite all attempts of the rival union and the mill owners and despite all the pressures from the govt. machinery, it kept on gathering strength and momentum.

One could not but admire the local communist leadership's role in upholding the strike.

Comrade Vinod had drained him off all his energy in roaming through the labourer-slums, in encouraging the slum-dwellers to participate in the strike, in collecting funds, in arousing the slogan "long live the red flag" and in roaming around the city in different rallies. After returning from work, he tiredly slept on a few pamphlets and on a piece of newspaper inside a small room of the party office. He fell deep asleep.

After some time Comrade Lalita entered the room. Comrade Lalita—a slim-figured, soft-spoken person and a good writer! Her responsibility was to evaluate all the English circulars and books of the party. She also worked as the editor of its weekly journal. Because of the strike, she was also given another responsibility—writing the bulletin.

This house was in fact Comrade Lalita's office. She came inside and switched on the light. A small table lied adjacent to the western window. There were papers lying on it, which were loaded with even more newspapers. On the wall were hanging three equal sized photographs—in the middle was Marx, on the left was Stalin and on the right, was Lenin.

There was an old calling bell lying there on the heap of paper on the table. Lalita pressed that bell three times with her finger.

The office boy Ramu came in. Ramu was also a comrade. The son of a labourer!

Lalita told: "Coffee."

Ramu left.

The beautiful moon had risen up in the outer sky. Towards the endpoint of the factory area, there was the party office. A zigzag red-pebbled road ran near the window. Sometimes one would find a bullock cart moving along that road whereas at other times, one could trace one or two passersby walking along. On the other side of the road, there laid an uneven rocky field that elongated towards the dusky line of the horizon.

The tranquil moments of that night were scented with the sweet fragrance of an unknown flower bloomed somewhere in the dark.

Lalita switched off the light inside the room with a mixed feeling of exhaustion and irritation.

One thin ray of the moonlight from outside fell on her lap. Every corner of her soul was delighted with an unspeakable fullness and contentment. She thought that the human history has seen many revolutions and many conflicts; but there could never be an end to this beautiful moon-blanched evening; there could never be a pause to this evening's immense spread of joy.

Lalita switched on the light again. Enjoying Nature's beauty was nothing but escapism—counter-revolutionary bourgeoisie luxury.

Comrade Vinod had started snoring loudly.

Lalita had not seen Vinod yet. She was surprised by the sound of the snoring and then looked at that direction. Vinod wore a pair of half-cleaned trousers and a half-shirt. On his feet were 'kabuli' sandals; and on his half-torn shirt, there were a party badge and the picture of a sickle and a hammer.

Ramu brought a cup of coffee. Lalita ordered for another cup. Ramu left.

Lalita did respect Vinod a lot for his leadership qualities and for his knowledge in Marxism. Vinod could easily recite all the important quotations from Marx during a simple conversation. Once Vinod had fallen in love with a girl and the girl had also reciprocated and the marriage was almost to be completed as per the Indian tradition. But the girl's father was an unadulterated bourgeoisie, anti-Marxist. He made it quite clear right at the beginning that he can tolerate his son-in-law becoming a disciple of Sri Chaitanya[46], but can never tolerate his allegiance to the sickle & hammer...

---

46   A Hindu religious leader of the 16th Century.

Vinod returned empty-handed. His disappointment was not for his failed courtship, but for the fact that the communist party lost a committed girl like Lila whose contribution for its growth and proliferation would have been immense. But even today Vinod does not forget to send party bulletins to Lila on a regular basis. Yet when any friend of his makes gentle fun of his failed courtship occasionally, Vinod retorts by quoting Marx that "nothing is being, everything is becoming" meaning "nothing is still, everything moves." In Marxist dialectics, a failed courtship is not something to be pitied.

Ramu brought another cup of coffee. Lalita woke up and tipped Vinod's forehead in a soft, girlish touch.

Vinod woke up, rubbed his eyes and sat on the newspaper heap.

Lalita asked: "Would you mind a cup of coffee, Comrade?"

Vinod's eyes and face lit up with the joy of some unexpected achievement.

He said: "Thank you Comrade."

Then both of them came and sat near the table. Lalita lifted the coffee cup onto her lips. And both started sipping coffee form their respective cups.

Outside, the blooming moon had spread its crimson light all around. On the other side of the road, was the uneven hinterland.

The pebbly field lied ahead. From there one could hear the intoxicating symphony of Raag Nageswari[47] from some body's flute.

---

47   -A classical musical note

Vinod asked; "Has tomorrow's bulletin gone to the press, Comrade Lalita?"

Lalita was thinking of a poem in her mind:

"O moon! Distances disappear between you and me!

You have come to me in new attire, my lover!

Come to my window O divine beauty!

Kiss me and hold me in your embrace!"

Vinod told: "Lalita! Arrangements are being made for a huge gathering tomorrow evening. From tomorrow onwards the other mill workers of the area are joining the mass strike. Your bulletin must be sharp and penetrative like a bullet. Could you please compose a chorus for tomorrow's meeting?"

Lalita asked with a lot of curiosity: "What kind of a song, Vinod? Would you clarify?'

"On a barren soil did you sprout

crops of gold—the crops of gold?"

Lalita started laughing loudly.

Vinod asked in an embarrassed voice: "Why did you laugh"?

Lalita abruptly answered: "No reason! I just laughed like that."

Vinod took out a cigarette from his pocket and lighted it.

Lalita looked at the portrait of Marx with a feeling of exhaustion and depression, and then said while addressing the portrait: "Hey Marx! Your *Economical Interpretation of History* has converted human beings into pigs. Life for him is all about bread and butter. You have taught man only to eat and eat and eat. In the eyes of man, you have made this piece of bread more beautiful than the moon. You have made money the ultimate goal of human life. But there is a greater goal for man than money. Have you ever spoken about that?"

Vinod threw that half-burnt cigarette out of the window and uttered in a grave voice: "I have been observing for quite some time comrade that you are becoming an escapist. Freud calls this escapism a death instinct—the gist of Buddhism. The tendency to lose yourself in a huge vacuum is nothing but a mental weakness, a bourgeoisie luxury, a spiritual stagnancy. In the words of Erick Fromm, it's the 'terrorism of freedom'."

Laita got a little irritated from inside. She could not at all tolerate these self-less, bookish machines. They think as if the words of Marx, of Freud, of Fromm are everything in life. Whatever lies outside their propositions is all weak, absurd, bourgeoisie luxury.

Lalita answered: "I have heard a lot of those, Comrade. Let's go outside. The moon looks wonderful."

Had it been another day, Vinod would have ridiculed Lalita's proposal calling it a counter- revolutionary bourgeoisie luxury or would have explained to her the in-depth tactics and principles of Lenin's coup d' art. Today what he looked for was indeed the night's cool and peaceful serenity after a whole day's hard toil.

Vinod said: "let's go."

Vinod and Lalita had walked a long way. The city was left much behind. Before them, there was the vast expanse of the uneven field, the pleasing fickleness of the moonlight.

Vinod and Lalita both sat on a hump of the soil.

Vinod kept on talking about the content of Marx's letter to Engel. Words kept bouncing from his mouth like parched rice bouncing on the frying pot.

Lalita asked with a sudden tone of sarcasm: "Hey Vinod! Has Marx not said something about such a beautiful, cool moonlight somewhere?"

Vinod kept pondering over an answer to this question when they could hear the magic symphony of somebody's flute in that sea of moonlight. The symphony mingled into that moonlit night that was spread all over the uneven field like a blanket. They were all becoming one. Lalita and Vinod listened to that music like two hypnotized beings.

Within no time, they could see the faint silhouettes of two human beings coming and sitting at a distance. There was no stopping of that flute's music. It was like a river spilling over its banks to fling itself into that sea of moonlight.

Both Lalita and Vinod were uncontrollably anxious to see those two human beings.

They came closer.

As they approached Lalita and Vinod, the music of the flute stopped. Lalita and Vinod recognized them— Nayana and Kajri. They were labourers of the mill that had gone on a strike. They were from Chhotnagpur.

Their wages were stopped due to the strike. Perhaps they had to spend the night without food. Yet, they were full of life's unlimited exuberance.

Lalita said: "You can play the flute beautifully, Nayana".

Nayana answered in her Chhatisgadi[48] dialect: "Yes sister! When the moon rises in our area, we start roaming in the hills and jungles."

---

48   A dialect spoken in Chhatishgarh, Madhya Pradesh.

The night was getting darker. Lalita and Vinod returned to their office.

Lalita kept thinking that the failure of Marxism lies here. Life is not all about production and distribution. Full wage and full belly may be the necessity of life, but not its ultimate goal. Then for whom are this luxury of the moonlight and the fullness of Nature? Life is more beautiful than mere living.

In the struggle and hullaballoo of living, Marxism had forgotten the beauty of life.

Lalita said: "Vinod! These two ladies are full of life."

Vinod jerked and then, looked at Lalita. He felt as if somebody hit him both soft and hard in the locked door of his heart. Nayana played her flute again. The fragrance of the Hina[49] flower in Kajri's wig mingled with the night.

Vinod lifted his eyes and looked at Lalita.

Bathed in moonlight, Lalita's body sparkled in an unforeseen resplendence. Vinod looked at her again with extreme keenness. But the next moment he thought it's all nothing but a meaningless bourgeoisie sentiment.

Nayana and Kajri were also coming back though the same uneven field.

Lalita had to go back to her room and write tomorrow's bulletin. Her body and mind became intoxicated with a feeling of exhaustion and irritation.

The music of Nayana's flute was getting dissolved in the night's brooding tranquillity.

---

49   A sweet-smelling sub-continental flower whose botanical name is Lawsonia Inermis.

It seemed to Lalita that the receding music was nothing but a wakeup call to Marxism and its theoretical propositions for the struggle for existence.

****

The False Capital

The alarm bell rang like someone's screeching scream: "Get up! It's seven in the morning . . ." Another day started. Subodh was always afraid of the day's beginning as it was going to be taxing. He stopped the clock's lever with a feeling of irritation. He wished it rang after fifteen minutes.

The morning light had not yet reached the room tearing the thick velvet veil of the night. Everything was a mixture of shades, of liquid darkness and faint light. On the table, the flower vase looked like a cluster of crumpled dreams. Subodh did not feel like sleeping anymore. He pressed the calling bell on the table for bed tea and the morning newspaper.

These two addictions were his morning needs. He required tea to reactivate his sleeping nerves. And he required the morning newspaper to involve in a mess of nonsense: whether our nation is able to produce aluminium as per its requirement or not, what the president of the United States of America told in the banquet-meeting, how many children are dying in Congo every day due to malnutrition, how fresh our prime minister looked yesterday morning, what are the chances of war with our neighbouring countries etc. These might have been questions relating to his professional life; but for him, these were futile and meaningless things in life. "Your profession burdens your life; but your life does not control your profession. This formula between your life and your profession is the real tragedy." Subodh told himself and continued: "I wish I looked into the matters of my kith and kin rather than looking into those in my surroundings. Today's newspaper is all about the life and the deeds of industrialists, underworld dons, a few self-styled monks, cricket players and film superstars. These news items do not cover the pains and pleasures of life. But there is intoxication in it."

But this was Subodh's profession . . . He was a special correspondent of a famous daily newspaper of the capital city.

Most of his time was spent in press conferences, in five star hotels in the midst of lunches, coffees and dinners. In the midst of all these, he kept typing his report in his typewriter.

But Subodh called these invitations meal-tickets and termed these conferences chicken soup free lunch sessions. But for these meal tickets, there was a lot of competition amongst his friends and colleagues.

Recently there was a congregation of a few national leaders in the capital. Amongst them, someone was a democratically elected leader; someone was a dictator and someone was a ruler whose rule might have ended anytime. Everybody was dancing to their tunes.

They were all invited to the capital to establish peace in the world. They did not have money, neither did they have arms and ammunitions; but they certainly had a collective voice that could create a global impact.

Subodh was in no way interested in this congregation and thought that it's better to see a cricket match on TV rather than listening to these national leaders and applauding their dresses, their cuisine, their style etc. on the close circuit TVs in the media center.

The editor however was a little annoyed with Subodh's characteristic nihilism and told: "It's a big assignment, Subodh. There is a lot of hue and cry over it. How can you be so cynical and reluctant about it? I am surprised."

Subodh answered: "There is no innovation in these assignments, Sir. And thus they don't attract me. As simple as that!"

"What do you mean?" Said the editor leaving a mouthful of smoke from his pipe. "This will be one of our biggest achievements as hosts."

Subodh answered back: "Sir! This country has seen so many farces like this. This is another one. Nothing new in this!"

The editor said: "You are a cynic Subodh! You always see the opposite side of things."

This allegation on Subodh on the editor's part was not entirely unfounded. If he could accept everything easily, he would have attained peace and happiness in life. But his life was full of such complications right from the beginning; nothing came to him easily and effortlessly. He had seen life's ugly face from close quarters and his bitter experiences had assumed the form of a psychosis, which he perhaps had inherited from his forefathers. A sinful attitude indeed!

Subodh further told the editor: "Sir! My cynicism has always helped you to comprehend things better, to estimate things correctly."

But for his quintessential cynicism, he had become an alien in his journalist community. One relishes being safe and protected inside a congregation and there was pain in aloofness, in standing alone on the top of a mountain and looking into the silence of the valley with the eye of a cynic. But Subodh perhaps relished being alone.

The conference of the national leaders had come to an end. Subodh's reporting was widely acclaimed and extensively admired. Even a press-attaché from the palace had congratulated Subodh on his reporting.

Subodh had taken complete leave for one week after the conference. Today was the last day of his leave.

He took a few sips from the cup and pulled his long hairs to break his sleep.

An engagement pad lied open near the bed-lamp close to the teapoy.

This capital was the city of many events — a symposium on poverty to be inaugurated by a minister at 11 am in the convention hall of the five star hotel Vikramaditya, a dinner party in the moonlight club, the birth day party of Santa Saxsena etc. A man without proper dresses and etiquettes had no place here. But Subodh only knew how hollow from the core was this elite culture? But still one had to succumb to such sophisticated requirements of high society. Otherwise, what was the requirement for him sending a flower bouquet along with birthday wishes to Santa Saxena? Subodh dialled a telephone number in Hotel Blue Diamond, ordered for a flower bouquet of orchids and roses and sent it to Santa Saxena's room. Then he spoke to her and wished her a very very happy birthday. Subodh imagined that she was holding the bouquet in her hands and pushing the orchid and rose clusters against her cheek and saying: "How lovely! How lovely!"

The paralysed Mr. Saxena looked at Santa while sitting on his wheel chair and told: "The bouquet looks fabulous. Only a lovely lady like you should own it." And then there was a little flicker of smile on his face.

Mrs. Saxena kissed her husband on his forehead and said: "O! How naughty you are!"

But was there a sensuous joy in that kiss? A heartfelt intimacy for the lover? An unquenched thirst of ages? Clearly, now it was not possible between them primarily because of their huge age-gap and also for the fact that Mr. Saxena was paralysed on his bed. Santa, though approaching forty, still looked young. Mr. Saxena had once given an advertisement in the news paper for a companion because he had become alone after his wife's death. Santa had carefully extracted all the information regarding how much of share Mr. Saxena held in big companies, how big was his bank balance, and how many palatial mansions he owned in different cities. The companionship ended in marriage.

That day Santa had come out in a certain pretext and Subodh had by chance met her inside a coffee house.

Subodh asked her in a carefully crafted, sentimental tone: "Santa! Are you really happy in this marriage?"

Santa took out a cigarette from her vanity bag and said: "Nobody is perfectly happy in this world under any circumstance, Subodh. It is only money and profit that matter. That is the law of our existence. Mental peace and happiness are only meaningless, old age words."

Subodh did not ask further. Santa's previous husband had divorced her. She also had a lot of material needs. Mr. Saxena was also living a very lonely life.

But why did Subodh need to poke his head into Santa's matters? A lot of women like her had come into his life like rainbows and had gone out.

Santa would also go like them.

The telephone rang. Someone asked: "Is it Subodh Kapoor speaking?"

There was a frown of irritation on his face. Again this boring character! The voice on phone said: "Hello Subodh! This is Professor Dr. Malhotra speaking."

Subodh answered in a clandestinely irritated voice: "What's the news?"

Professor Dr. Malhotra! It was all a hoax. This Malhotra was a mere lecturer in a private college once. Now he calls himself Professor Dr. Malhotra. In this capital, who cares for in which subject you have completed your Ph. D.? What was your thesis?

Malhotra was a huge hoax. But in today's politics, these hoaxes topped the list of successful people in the society.

Prof. Dr. Malhotra said: "Subodh! We sat together once a few days back. Let's sit today again. I have a nice thing for you."

Subodh did understand what is the meaning of a nice thing? A nice thing meant foreign liquor. Dr. Malhotra was the union president of the fourth class employees of the foreign embassies. Through them, he could arrange such 'nice things' quite easily, that too without any cost.

But the danger that lied in accepting his invitation was that at the end of the drink he would tell you to send a report on something to the newspaper and then, publish it. A eulogy on the foreign minister, for instance! And then he would say: "The foreign minister is visiting the United Sates this week end. This statement should be flashed in the newspaper before his departure." And after finishing off four pegs of whiskey offered by him for free, one could hardly refute his request. Like a letterhead company, Professor Malhotra was a leader in the newspapers. Sometimes he could even send you in a foreign visit either in a friendship association or in some delegation. He was either the president or the secretary of half-a-dozen friendship associations.

But Professor Malhotra and a few more like him never understood how meanly the foreign diplomats of the embassy looked at them for their cheap greed for free scotch and whiskey. They thought that these people could be easily bought and sold for a few bottles of whiskey. And they could lobby for their own interests through these easily buyable and sellable people. Theses sycophants were everywhere . . . from the palace to the parliament.

Sycophancy and nepotism were the fundamental principles of the capital city's politics. The bigger a sycophant you were, the more successful a politician you were.

Professor Malhotra asked on the telephone: "Why do you keep quiet Subodh?"

"We will sit together another day, professor. There is an urgent engagement this evening." Said Subodh and kept the receiver in an irritated way.

After the end of today's symposium, there was still ample time left in the hand. Subodh told himself: "I can go a little late to Santa's dinner party tonight and spend that time sipping whiskey in Professor Malhotra's house. But he was also overawed by Professor Malhotra's oily behaviour that at times looked awkward and terribly inconvenient.

Pretension and deception were the mental features of the city politicians. They pretended about the greatness of their leadership qualities in the newspapers. That was their satisfaction.

This Professor Malhotra was a strange creature. To give attendance in the palace was his everyday work though it was not always possible for him to move inside and meet the diplomat. But once upon a time he had some sort of closeness with him. The latter once told him, perhaps out of a friendly intimacy, that he can go a long way in life. Capitalising on that, Professor Malhotra declared outside that he is an important person of the palace. He also declared in his friend-circle that the honourable diplomat intends to make him the corporator of a big city. The news also reached the other sycophants around the diplomat. They got jealous and tried very tactfully to instigate him against the professor. On one occasion when Professor Malhotra was coming back after presenting a flower bouquet to the diplomat, one of the latter's acolytes told him directly in a very clear and unambiguous voice: "Mr. Professor! People in the palace are not particularly liking your regular entry into the palace. It's better if you come less." Professor Malhotra immediately understood the gesture behind such words and gradually, his entry into the palace was getting restricted. And it did not take him long to understand that the real diktat was from the diplomat, in a clandestine manner though for he never told things directly to anybody. He always passed the information to the targeted person through his acolytes. Even Prof. Malhotra was also doing this job in the past. So he could understand the indications even better. But of course, he was certainly not the person who would give up so easily. He could not live for a moment leaving the palace forever. He kept on circling around it day in and day out. Many such people like him operated the similar way. Intimacy with the palace was their armour. That is precisely why despite being rejected by its administration, Professor Malhotra never stopped going there.

But even if Professor Malhotra could not meet the diplomat anymore, he did not get disappointed and exhausted. These days, he stands beneath a mango tree inside the palace and welcomes the visitors with an expression of utmost seriousness on his face, as if he has been employed there to welcome them. While he welcomes the visitors, one can always trace on his face a serene smile of Lord Buddha and while greeting the people, he lifts his right hand in a posture of blessing. This style of greeting has become very popular in the capital city though nobody knows where it came from. Amongst the visitors are usually the rich people, businessmen and industrialists from different places and everybody who comes inside the palace knows Prof. Malhotra in some way or other. And Professor Malhotra tells them: "You please go inside. Meet the diplomat inside. I am always at your service." Professor Malhotra is a master in the art of speaking and is an inspiration for the visitors. Nobody gets disappointed with him. The visitors become overwhelmed with his warm welcome. This ability to act the way he does is his strength. With this ability of his, he has not only acquainted himself with the politicians of the capital city, but also has been able to procure large scale donations from the industrialists. This acting, this self-deception carries for him the very essence of his life. This is the principle of living for many of his likeminded people for whom meeting their own selfish purposes is everything in life. The goal of their political life is very limited—to earn money and power. There is no question of the idea of serving the people or serving the better interest of the nation in them. They are only for giving slogans. But when it comes to the question of fulfilling their own selfish interests, they can even sell the nation for that.

Self-aggrandisement in the media is an essentiality for people like Professor Malhotra. But for that of course they have to arrange a lot of good things (branded liquor) for the journalists. But of course, it is not a big thing for the president of the fourth class employees of the embassy to smuggle a few branded liquor bottles outside the palace. Professor Malhotra is an expert in this business. Even his biggest enemies would accept it.

But it was also becoming increasingly irritating for Subodh to publish Professor Malhotra's statements in the newspaper for a few pegs of whiskey, a chancellor cigarette packet and a cheap dinner. But Professor Malhotra was in no mood to leave Subodh. He telephoned him again: "Subodh! If you do not come, the evening will be spoiled." Subodh answered with clenched teeth and an expression of irritation on his face: "Sorry! Thanks."

No! Even he can also not go to Devinder Singh's breakfast anymore. Of course, he was also not willing to go there. This Devinder Singh is also another character in the capital city. He is a sub-agent in a European military aircraft manufacturing company. A lobby is required for selling aircrafts and for a lobby, one requires clandestine negative advertisement against other competing aircraft manufacturing companies. And for this one needs the cooperation of many — starting from parliament members to the journalists. And that is why it is a regular thing for Subodh to get invited to breakfasts, lunches or dinners into Devinder Singh's Jorbag palace. But slowly he has started disliking this business of sycophancy. He telephoned Devinder Singh and conveyed to him that he is extremely sorry for not being able to come to his breakfast invitation.

Then he got busy in his preparation for a symposium on poverty in Hotel Bikramaditya.

Poverty is another weapon in the hands of these cunning politicians of the capital city and its removal is the only concern for the people starting from the economists to the sycophants of this palace. But these people are all dressed in costly suits. And in their pockets are 'India King' cigarette packets. They all drive big, imported cars on the road. These are this era's new feudalists; but in their mouths there is always the slogan: "Remove poverty." This is of course another dimension of the self-deceiving practices in the capital city. This idea of removing poverty from the nation is not a new concept. In every nation there are some politicians who have perennially desired to accumulate power in their hands and 'poverty-removal' has always remained their favourite slogan. For, there is no better euphonic slogan than this in the world of politics. Poverty-ridden people are the largest community in many nations. Through these slogans, these politicians will at least get their support and it hardly matters whether the latter's poverty is removed or not. Leaders like Napoleon and Mussolini were also experts in these slogans; but even their nations have not gotten themselves completely rid of poverty. National poverty is indeed an advantage for these power-lobbying politicians. If it will go, then they will struggle to establish their political clout. As long as there is poverty in the society, these people will continue to thrive. After acquiring lots of wealth, they throw a little to the poor to get them to their side. But this does not remove poverty, rather makes it even more acute.

In this game of politics, the renowned economists are also big players and they have become famous by writing voluminous research books on poverty. Whether poverty is removed or not, their name and fame keeps on growing bigger day by day. Symposiums must be conducted for these people and the venues for such symposiums must be the air-conditioned convention halls of the five star hotels. The participants are all well-dressed with safari-suits and ties; they hold attachés while some others hold red-ribbon-bound files in their hands and they all hastily get down from imported cars and rush to the hotel poaches as if they cannot tolerate even a moment of poverty anywhere in the country. Some of these famous economists come and inaugurate symposiums and deliver impassionate talks on poverty to the audience. After the inaugural session gets over, you have the coffee sessions. Before they share their invaluable views on poverty with the audience, these subject-experts wet their throats with hot coffee. But without this, as if their words would get stuck in their throats. After the coffee session, there are one or two sessions for paper presentations followed by panel discussions on the subject and then there is lunch break. In the afternoon, there are few more paper-presentation-sessions followed by panel discussions and then the symposium comes to an end.

But despite such symposiums, poverty stretches its body outside like that of a long python. Even Subodh developed a terrible hatred for such meaningless symposiums. He gets surprised over how he is increasingly becoming such a terrible cynic these days?

If his vehicle's carburettor did not trouble him, Subodh could have reached the symposium in time. But when he entered the hall after checking in at the reception counter, only a few minutes after the esteemed leader's speech had passed. The audience was applauding his talk with incessant clapping. The great leader had told something extremely valuable.

A costly safari-suit-clad gentleman came onto the stage, stood in a dramatic posture, threw back a few hairs from his forehead and started talking about the definition of poverty. He said: "If poverty is not correctly defined right at the beginning, then all endeavours for its removal would be tantamount to swimming in fog. All the discussions going on in different developed and developing countries are in fact futile exercises as long as the very idea of poverty is not correctly defined. One should not become too pessimistic in these matters and a high level committee must be constituted by the symposium to first correctly define poverty." Then the gentleman went on and on and after finishing his speech, he gracefully took his seat.

There was a huge round of applause and the gentleman thought that it was an emotional expression of the audience's appreciation of his talk. Even the esteemed leader greeted him with a benevolent smile on his face for the invaluable speech he gave. However the gentleman failed to understand that the audience's clapping was not for any genuine appreciation of his talk, but rather was a purely customary thing, a mere reflex action. Whoever sits in the symposium has to clap like this along with others. The gentleman clearly failed to understand this.

The second speaker looked like a rebel—Professor Roshan Lal. A very well known face in the leftist circle! He is a faculty of Sociology in a very reputed educational institution dominated by leftist orientations. He wore a thick 'khadad' trouser and Punjabi and in his eyes were a pair of thick-framed zero-power spectacles. From his shoulders hung a Santiniketan-bag. A beard on his chin along with the deep, frowning lines on his forehead attributed to him the precious and sophisticated look of an intellectual. Professor Lal took out his thesis from his bag and again kept it inside and then, started his speech in a slow and calculated voice which however turned fiery and vigorous within moments like lava emanating from a volcano: "Whatever the previous speaker said is nothing but the repetitions of the voices of the capitalists, of the multinational company owners." Then this gentleman continued with his speech whose essence was that unless these exploitative capitalists are removed from this nation, poverty alleviation can never be achieved; it will rather go on increasing. The gentler man was greeted by the audience with another huge round of applause.

Now it was ten minutes to one o' clock.

Everybody was busy with lunch.

It was 3 o' clock and the lunch was over—a lunch that had five courses of different items.

In the afternoon session, came to speak Professor Lakdiwala—noted Gandhian economist. This gentleman was also opposed to the nation's capitalists, but for a different reason though. In his opinion, the only route to poverty-alleviation is the adoption of village-economy and promotion of small scale industries. For him, the nation requires no power plants. Cow-dung-gas would suffice. As long as there is 'charkha[50],' what is the need of a textile plant? Gandhiji of course had gone up to a single stitching machine. Not more than that! Of course, looking at the vastness of the nation, one might need trains and aeroplanes. But why would one need these sophisticated things in a competition-less village economy?

Professor Lakdiwala, keeping in tune with his communist ideology, wore a pair of motor-tyre-made shoes, a 'khadad' dhoti that ran up to his knees, a half-shirt, a long beard below his chin and a pair of looking glasses on his eyes. He was completely bald-headed, but never hesitated to speak and act in dramatic manners whenever necessary and spoke his mind without any inhibition. He started his speech:

"Poverty is nothing but a thinking. It has nothing to do with economy. You won't find a village in our country from where a guest will come back in empty stomach. Families, who cannot afford to eat meal twice a day, will also arrange a meal for the guest. Such mental richness makes them survive in the midst of all the poverty we have at hand. In the name of alleviating poverty, if their mental richness is removed from them, then the real poverty will never go away; rather these people will become mentally impoverished."

Prof. Lakdiwala went on and on...

---

50   -An indigenous, wooden tool to weave clothes. It was used by the father of the nation Mahatma Gandhi to do the same.

But perhaps his speech did not touch anybody's mind. After it got over, of course, one or two people gave a few customary claps. But it was also an indication of the fact that many people, who did not clap, did not agree to his ideas.

The participants were looking at their watches in worried gestures. After taking heavy lunches, they did not have the patience to listen to another boring speech on poverty.

Subodh also did not have that patience. He came out of the discussion hall. For him, it was all sheer wastage of time and a fake show of intellectuality.

He typed the report in the newspaper room in the evening. In his report, he highlighted the speeches and statements of Professor Lakdiwala; but his writing was in fact an acute and fierce criticism of such fake drama going on in the nation in the name of intellectual discussions on poverty. However, the news editor put huge red and blue crosses on his writing and told him: "If you continue to do like this, then you will be very soon fired by your boss. So be careful Mr. Subodh." Subodh answered: "He is most welcome to do that."

Outside, the evening had grown denser. The roads were looking different in gas light. He did not feel like going back to his flat and changed his dresses for Santa Acharya's birthday party. He parked his car outside a garden and went inside to sleep flat on its grassy lawn and to kill the day's boredom by looking at the starry night sky. He ran his fingers through his grey hair and told himself: "Even this will do."

At least there is no faking in the slow wind of the evening and in the darkness of the night.

While driving his car into the golden premises of No. 3 Moonlight Colony, Subodh felt has he not reached in a wrong address? No-This is No. 3 Moonlight Colony. He was too well-acquainted with it. To clear the doubts of his mind, he stopped his vehicle in the midway and looked at the roadside Eucalyptus trees. No! He had not made any mistake. Today was Santa Saxena's birthday party. Below the portico was her imported Limousine car and neither any other vehicle nor a human being was visible inside such a huge premise. The big compound and the duplex looked completely empty. The bright halogens outside the glass windows and doors had intensified the tranquillity of the surrounding. "But where has everybody gone?" Subodh asked himself.

He came out of his car in a disturbed manner when he met a uniform-wearing servant on the veranda. The servant saluted him.

Subodh asked: "What is the matter? Why others have not arrived yet?"

The servant answered: "The invitation was at 8.30."

Subodh looked at his wrist watch and was surprised to find that it has stopped at 8.30. Something had gone wrong with it.

He was a little disturbed that he has missed the party. To relieve his tension, the servant told him in a softened voice: "Please go to the drawing room inside. Sir (Santa's husband) is resting there."

There was no use going back. Subodh went inside. The drawing room was empty. Another servant was cleaning the sofa and the centrepieces with a broom. Another one was decorating the flower vases with different-shaped flowers. Subodh was not an unknown figure in this place. The servants greeted him with salutes and requested him to sit.

But Subodh was very restless. He asked: "Where is madam?"

He knew he will meet Santa in some gathering in a party somewhere. But if he meets her today alone on her birthday in this tranquil moment, he will definitely take her by a pleasant surprise. There is an excitement in giving her such surprises.

Someone answered: "Madam is inside her bedroom."

Today Subodh wants to give a surprise to Santa. As if it is the most precious gift for her on her birthday. He walked stealthily on the carpeted stairs towards Santa's bedroom on the upper storey.

Santa had not closed the door from inside. The light inside the room was sparsely visible to the outside through the thin fissures between the door and the door screen. Subodh's eyes lit up with naughtiness. He thought Santa would be ecstatic to see him alone near her after such a long time. He lifted the curtain slightly from outside and peeped inside the room.

Santa was sitting on a small mahogany chair in front of her dressing mirror. She looked lost inside herself. Looking at her own image in the mirror, she had perhaps forgotten her situation and environment. She looked frozen to stillness just like the cosmetic bottles and boxes on the dressing table. It looked as if she was hypnotized by her own image on the mirror.

Before taking a new make-up, Santa had gotten

herself rid of all the previous make-ups. Beneath the make-up, laid concealed the many wrinkles on her face, the many scars of her growing age, the many frowns beneath her two eyes and finally, her unavoidable ugliness.

It was a terrible revelation for Subodh to see Santa without make-up. Her bob-cut hair was the envy of many women; it was the attraction and adoration for her male friends like Subodh; it was the insignia of her glowing youth and beauty. But O God! What was this? It was a wig. Subodh could not believe his eyes. The wig was lying on the dressing table like a dead thing.

Santa had already become bald-headed. The baldness of her head sparkled with electric light. Some scattered locks of hair hanged form here and there from her head. She was looking like a ghost. Even her curvy eyebrows were fake. She had decorated them with her hands.

Subodh stealthily walked down the stairs. It looked as if he had no strength in his feet, neither did he have the old excitement to join Santa's birthday party.

It seemed to him as if Santa Saxena was the true insignia of the capital city's pretensions.

****

The Wandering Gypsy

I

A thorough and refined gentleman! He has a handsome monthly earning. He has a decent family life with his wife and son. His bank balance has increased of late; but along with it has also increased his body fat. And along with them have also come dyspepsia, diabetes and blood pressure. This family life has given him pleasure. Oh!... While shaving, his blade slipped off. Kamal started bleeding. Oh! This growing age gives nothing but pain; it gives you death every moment. Kamal was bleeding from his chin.

He took out his handkerchief to wipe off the blood from his chin. The silken handkerchief emitted the fragrance of 'evening-in-Paris' perfume. Mallika told she will come today. Kamal, half-shaved, got up, went to the door and locked it from outside. He lifted the half-broken railing of the window and came back into the room, and washed his face with soap. Then he emitted a long, deep sigh of relief. It was a beautiful idea. He could always lock the room from outside and sleep peacefully inside. By doing so, he could fully avoid the house owner, the mixture-seller, Mallika and everybody else as they would think that Kamal is absent for the room is locked from outside. Kamal lifted the half-broken railing of the window and came into the room, and washed his face with soap. Then he emitted a long, deep sigh of relief. It was a wonderful idea; he could always lock the room from outside and sleep peacefully in his room.

****

Kamal travelled back in time through the memory lane.

That day Mallika was sleeping on his chest in the secluded corner of a park. Kamal said: "Mallika! I don't believe in love. A man does not have emotions; he does not have sentiments; he does not have soft feelings. He believes only in one basic, primitive instinct. Love is his incarceration, marriage is his confinement. But woman needs love. For that, she needs a man. That's why she loves her man and loves him more than her life. But for a man love is nothing but surrender. And I hate surrender, Mallika. I hate surrender."

Mallika said; "You are a cruel man, Kamal! You are a cruel man. You know Kamal! How much I have suffered by falling in love with you? What terrible pain I have undergone?

Mallika's gown was full of the 'bloomed-lotus' embroidery.

She was a sub-inspector in the Police Department. She was chubby, dusky-complexioned, big-toothed.

****

Nine o' clock in the morning. On a plane sheet of paper, Kamal scribbled the whole day's routine. He had to catch hold of that rascal Basant first.

Kamal took out a cigarette from the ash tray and lighted it.

He met Basant and they engaged in a conversation. Kamal said; "Basant! You are not only stupid, you are a big moron. Hey idiot! You were giving singing-tuition to some students and were earning something, and that was your earning for the whole month. Now you have left that. Then how would you manage your expenses?"

Basant said: "O! That is true. I had not yet thought of it. But Kamal! If there is no vigour of life here, then how can there be music? Why are these girls learning music? Sometimes I feel like getting asphyxiated before these girls. Ok . . . Can you lend me twenty rupees? The house owner is a monster. He has confiscated my harmonium. Now he eyes on my table."

Basant threw his long hair towards the back of his head.

****

It has been six months since then. There is no news of Mr. Basant. Gone are also those borrowed twenty rupees.

Kamal said to himself: "Today I have to catch hold of the other fellow, Sripati Babu. Sripati Chaudhry! Lake Road! What is today's date? Monday! In which nostril I am breathing right now? Left nostril! Breathing in the left nostril on Monday! It's a positive premonition. Hey Mother Kali! Hey Mother Shyama! I wish Sripati Chaudhury does a life insurance policy with me today. I heard he is ready for an insurance policy of one lakh rupees. I will enjoy its commission for the whole year. . . . Oh God! This coat has lost its iron and has become wrinkled. But it's still manageable. . . . But where is Mallika? The ugly Mallika? Ugly both in body and mind! But what is the harm in marrying her? It does not matter even if she has a hundred affairs. Still she has a body that can be enjoyed. Her body is good enough."

It was already eleven. No! There was no news of Mallika. Kamal wiped off his face with that handkerchief. The fragrance of the 'evening-in-Paris' perfume was right in his nostrils.

II

Oh shit! Kamal hit a boulder. His boot-sole cracked at the right corner. This rascal road-corporation! The whole road is full of boulders and potholes. Nobody bothers if half of your foot goes. You will get some iodine and some cotton from the nearby dispensary and your injury will slowly heal. But at least hundred rupees will be required to repair this cracked sole. It's actually the cost of a cigarette packet. It also means ten tension-free dreamy moments. Or else, four cups of special tea!

The next street is the fish-market-street. Then there is the Broadway Restaurant.

Below the coat, there is a beast with huge canines. Hunger!

Kamal said to himself: "I need a cup of tea. Yes! Only one cup of tea! My nerves have become dormant. One cup of tea is five rupees. One pack of cigarette is hundred rupees. The bus fare is twenty rupees. But I have only hundred rupees in my pocket. It's better to walk to Sripati Chaudhury on foot. "

Kamal started walking...

III

A big road! Some cobbler was calling: "Shoe-polish

Sir! Shoe polish! Don't you need shoe-polish, Sir? Don't you need it? Your sole is cracked sir. Your sole is cracked. Your right finger is visible through the crack, Sir."

Kamal kept on walking heedlessly. After a few steps there will be the fish market.

He reached the number 3 fish market. But where is Mr. Basant Das? The door is locked. On a bench at a distance, the pea-seller Mr. Khan is sitting and sipping tea from a cup. "Perhaps he is also waiting for Basant. Oh God! I won't be able to meet this Basant. This rascal has escaped." Kamal said to himself.

"Then I must meet Sripati Chaudhury. But again, his house is four miles away." Thought Kamal.

"Oh! Here comes Basant's house owner. He can give me some information about Basant." Kamal said to himself.

Basant's house owner greeted Kamal with a hello and said: "Good evening Kamal Babu. Look at this Basant Babu. A thorough gentlemen! But see! He has not paid my house rent for months together."

Kamal answered: "Where is Basant Babu? I am also searching for him."

The house owner answered: "He has absconded. I have taken away his harmonium. Now he has vanished after throwing his table in a corner of my house. He told me he is getting married and he will clear all my rents after marriage."

"Basant's marriage? When is he getting married? That day Mallika was also telling about a marriage." Kamal told himself.

****

That day Mallika told Kamal: "Kamal! We will build our dream-home away from the din and bustle of the city. You and me, a small house, a greenery-filled hill at the back and a river in the front!" On another evening also, Mallika came to Kamal with the same marriage proposal, with the same dream talk.

Kamal told her with an intention to hurt: "Mallika! How many dream-homes have you constructed with other men before me?"

Mallika is a strange creature. She can easily take any offence with a smiling face. She has forgotten her past; now she wants a family even at the cost of pain, humiliation and suffering. That day Mallika's wig was decorated with beautiful red flowers. Red flowers on a black wig . . .

Mallika told while answering to Kamal's questions; "Kamal! Body and soul are two different things. I have looked for that soul in many bodies. But today, I have lost the beauty of this body at the age of thirty five. What attraction will you find in this worn-out body of mine? But today I have come with the attraction of the soul."

There was the sweet and beautiful fragrance of the 'evening-in-Paris' perfume in Mallika's body.

Kamal said: "Mallika! You and me are far away from the main town, in a tranquil bamboo-covered village. On all sides, there are sprawling fields after fields merging into the sky. Let's enjoy the beauty of Nature."

Mallika left after some time.

Kamal said to himself: "There is a peace in this surrender. There is no shame, no torture, no humiliation in self-protection. Basant has taken the right track. Nobody can escape from the society. There is no point fighting with the opposite sex. There is absolute peace and bliss in this surrender. This fight is meaningless. Om Shanti! Shanti! Shanti! This is wasteland . . . Above is the sprawling, blue sky."

IV

A little distance away!

After taking a right turn from the Motiganj Street, there is the Chaudhury Mansions. Sripati Chaudhury's Mansions! The blessed 'son of destiny! He can make an insurance of at least one lakh rupees. Kamal offered him a cigarette. Mr. Chaudhury said: "No thanks!" While trying to persuade him for the insurance, Kamal said: "See Mr. Chaudhury! Great poet Bharati has said: "Nalini Dalagata Jalamati Taralang. Life is like a tiny water drop on a lotus leaf." Bharati? Or Magha? Or Bana? Or Kalidasa? Or Sankaracharya? Kamal could not recollect. But he continued; "You must have heard Mr. Chaudhury that in America, the girls insure even the moles on their cheeks. Even the hair in their heads!" Kamal's voice looked convincing and persuasive.

Then he put a cigarette in his mouth and lighted it to rejuvenate his body and mind. The prolonged dusk of the last spring! There were rows of Devdaru[51] trees on both sides of Lake Road. It looked as if the whole world was sleeping. There was no street vendor, no 'shoe-polish-shouting' cobbler, no noise. Only, small piles of fallen Devdaru leaves all along! Here there was no obstacle, no pothole... Here, the motion of the universe was smooth and uncomplicated. A motor cycle raced past Kamal. The

---

51   A thin-sub-continental tree with long flowers.

Devdaru leaves flew into the air for a moment and then fell scattered on the ground.

There was the huge 'Chaudhury Mansions' right in front. A Ghurkha[52] durwan[53] was dozing near the gate. Kamal stretched his coat with his hands to make it look ironed. The horn of a motor vehicle was heard from inside. The Ghurkha durwan got up from his sleep with a jerk. He squeezed a bamboo stick beneath his shoulder, stood up and saluted to the man sitting inside the car and then, opened the iron-gate. A huge black-coloured car went out. Left behind were whirlpools reddish dust and dry Devdaru leaves.

"What do you want?" Asked the Ghurkha durwan to Kamal sitting on his chair. The irritation was visible on his face for his sleep was disturbed.

Kamal told in a slow voice with clenched teeth: "I want your head." The durwan obviously did not hear it. While lighting a half-burnt 'bidi[54],' he said: "Sahib just went out. You cannot meet him today."

Kamal felt like smacking the durwan on his dilated nose.

V

Again a long, stretching road of five miles back! Kamal's legs were paining. He has to go back and give it another try the next day. There were only ten rupees left in his pocket. Of course, he has to come by bus tomorrow. The bus fare will be four rupees.

---

52   A Nepali and Indian tribe.
53   Indian colloquial term for watchman.
54   A thin smoking pipe containing tobacco inside. It is smoked by many people who are addicted to tobacco smoke.

Someone threw a lot of ground-nut-chaffs on him from above. In the approaching darkness of the evening, Kamal looked at the man sitting on the wall nearby. Someone was happily chewing ground nuts sitting on that wall. Kamal felt like dragging that man's feet and then, throwing him on the ground. In the meanwhile, the man jumped onto the ground from the wall. In the dim street light, Kamal could see that he was no other than his friend Vinod, standing in a stylish posture with a packet of ground nuts in his hand.

Kamal asked: "What were you doing on that wall Vinod?"

Vinod answered in a taunting voice: "I was performing yoga."

Kamal asked: "What do you mean?"

Vinod said: "I mean yoga. I can see past, present and future, Kamal. I know you went to meet Sripati Chaudhury to make a life insurance for him. Right? But before you have just reached his house, he went on in his Packard car for an evening ride. Right?

Kamal asked in a surprised tone: "How could you know this, man?

Vinod answered in a sympathetic voice: "Hey! I was watching it all from this wall. The moment you approached the gate of 'Chaudhury Mansions,' he went out in his car for an evening ride. I was watching it all from here. Then after getting a kick from the durwan, you are coming back with a downcast head. Isn't it right my friend? If you did not want a life insurance policy from him, then why would you have gone there? This is all sheer common sense my friend, sheer common sense. You do not need to be a rocket scientist to understand this."

Kamal asked: "But Vinod! What was the need for you to come so long from five miles away to sit on this wall and chew ground nuts?"

Vinod looked at him and smiled and then, both started walking together.

Vinod pushed the pack of ground nuts into Kamal's hand and said: "It's big, sad news bother. You know Mallika. She is a sub-inspector in the Police Department and gets a salary of two hundred rupees per month and also free lodging. A free, independent and healthy life! I had proposed her to marry me. Let her be above thirty five! Let her be ugly-looking . . ."

Kamal added: "Let her be thin-breasted, dark-complexioned, tall-toothed . . ."

Vinod said: "If I married her, all my problems would have been solved. I could have easily completed my research project on 'primitive human culture' without any financial difficulty."

Kamal asked: "But why would Mallika want to marry a 'good-for-nothing' creature like you?"

Vinod answered: "Hey idiot! This whole Earth runs on the principle of relativity. Everything is relative here. I may be a 'good-for-nothing' creature for you. But I am precious for Mallika. You know what she told me? She says: "Vinod! I have come with the beauty of my soul for you. My body has lost all its attraction at thirty five."

Kamal asked in an injured voice: "Then what? What did she say more?

Vinod said: "No! She said nothing more. I was till now hiding from her, from the appeal of her soul. But now when

I have decided to marry her, I hear that she has already gotten married."

Kamal felt like falling from the sky and asked with an anxious voice: "Mallika has gotten married! When? To whom?"

Vinod answered: "I don't know when. But I know she has married that vagabond Basant Das. He was teaching her Sitar. That is when their romance started and then, he has married her. They have left the town yesterday somewhere for honeymoon."

Kamal said to himself: "Oh God! Everything is lost. My last hope for Mallika is also gone. With that also is gone the hope of getting back twenty rupees from that rascal Basant. Now if I ask him that money, he will answer: "That money is your gift for our marriage." Then also, Kamal has already looted a lot of money from Mallika. But still, he thought this might be an opportunity for a life insurance for Basant. He thought he will go to Basant and tell: "See Basant! I am telling all this to you as your well-wisher. Now you are into family life. There are lots of responsibilities in family life, but there are also possibilities of mishaps in life. So, to keep the destiny of your family secured, you must do a life insurance for yourself."

Kamal discovered another thorn in his sole. It was now impossible for him to walk any more with his shoes on. He lifted a piece of paper from the road, kept his shoes in it and started walking with naked feet.

Vinod told Kamal: "Now do you understand friend? Why I was sitting on that wall and chewing ground-nuts, far away from the din and bustle of the city? I was doing so out of pure grief. I was cursing the universe for the torture that it has inflicted on me."

But Kamal could not so easily forgive that rascal Basant inside his mind. Buffoon! He did not give me my twenty rupees. And again, he has also married Mallika secretly, without even informing any of us.

In the front, there was a restaurant.

One gets very tasty prawn cutlets here. There was the beautiful fragrance of prawn cutlet in the wind. Both the friends started smelling it. Kamal carefully scrambled for money in his pocket. The cruel beast of hunger had already started gnawing his belly from inside.

Vinod placed his hand on Kamal's shoulder and said; "Come friend! We are feeling very hungry."

Both of them got into the restaurant without wasting further time. First Vinod, then Kamal! Both sat near a table in the corner.

Vinod hit the table in his hand and called the restaurant-boy in a heavy voice: "Boy! Boy!"

Kamal said in a timid voice: "There is not a single rupee in my pocket, friend. There is not a single coin there."

Vinod said; "It's not easy to fool me Kamal! I have heard the jingling sound of coins in your pocket. Now you see what is in my pocket."

Vinod took out his two pant pockets. Some ground nuts came out from them and fell on the ground.

Kamal cursed Vinod in a voice with clenched teeth— shirker, idiot, dacoit, rascal. In the name of friendship, you called me to this restaurant and now you want to rob me off the last traces of my treasure.

By that time, the half-pant wearing restaurant-boy had already come to the table and was waiting for the orders.

Kamal told in a helpless voice: "Four prawn cutlets."

A Hindi gazal[55] was playing inside the restaurant. Vinod started singing keeping in tune with the song that was playing.

The restaurant-boy came back with two prawn-cutlets in each plate and placed them on the table. Vinod put one cutlet into his mouth and started chewing it like a wild animal.

VI

The friends came out of the restaurant and lighted their respective cigarettes.

Kamal asked: "What next?"

Vinod answered while leaving a mouthful of smoke into the air: "The journey is aimless and also, endless."

Kamal remembered his dilapidated rented house in that dirty slum. The house-owner must be sitting on the veranda waiting for him for the rent and would be twisting his moustache to kill time. Once this image floated in his mind, all his courage to go back to the rented house vanished into the air like smoke.

Echoing Vinod's words, Kamal told: "Truly friend! The journey is aimless."

Vinod dragged one of Kamal's arms towards one street and said: "I am very tired friend."

Kamal asked: "But where? You cannot enter the park at 12 o' clock in the night. The police will arrest us and we have finally to spend time in the police station."

Vinod answered: "No! It's not the park. It's the refugee camp in front."

---

55   A kind of Indian classical song.

VII

The refugee camp!

Initially, it was somebody's jute 'go down.' It was a huge asbestos-covered hall where forty families had taken shelter. It was terribly hot inside. Therefore, forty small families were sleeping outside in the field, to get the cool, soothing breeze of the evening. Forty furnaces were burning out there. One furnace for one family! Somewhere boiled rice was getting separated from the boiling water; somewhere ladies were kneading breads. Along with that, there were the sounds of babies crying, the old folks shouting and the bangles of the ladies jingling. Vinod slept on a mat folding with both his hands beneath his head. Kamal also placed the coat below his head carefully for the fear of its ironing getting destroyed. Oh! It was so peaceful. The calm, soothing evening breeze! Millions of smiling stars in the sky! And the stealthily approaching darkness! From a distance was audible the din and bustle of the city.

At some distance away, a lady was kneading the bread and then, warming it in the fire. Around her, her four siblings were looking at her like hungry puppies. In the light of that fire, her thin and scraggy face looked clearer. She looked as the living statue of tolerance.

Vinod thought: "I have lost one relation. I need not be sad and broken. I will build another relation, another house. Man has survived through all bad lucks, all curses, and will continue to survive through them."

That lady took out one bread from the pot, made it into four parts and gave one to each of her four siblings, and then, put another bread on fire.

Vinod had started snoring.

VIII

Kamal has also slept.

You can these people vagabonds. You can call them beggars. No issues...

Vinod has slept. But if he was awake, he would have got up and told:

"I have researched into the whole of the human history from the old stone-age till today and found out that those who have not surrendered to the society and have remained aloof, have always suffered. Sadness, bad luck, humiliation and pain have been their eternal companions. But they have always searched for innovation and held to the society the light of newness. And in that light, the world has always rediscovered its identity. They may be the cursed human beings. The thin-breasted ugly Krishnas and Mallikas have come to their houses with the appeal of their souls. But these people have run away. You may call them lunatics, vagabonds."

But Vinod has always found evidence in support of these people from History.

Vinod has slept.

Kamal's snoring has become louder.

The lady has finished preparing her breads. Her four siblings have already slept.

****

The Last Remnant of Flood

Govind Pattanaik! An old man! With folded knees, he sat on the ground and kept looking at the flood water all around. The water stretched beyond his eyes. Two rivers "Keluni" and "Baghuni" had joined to make this devastating flood. There were only unfathomable grey, water, brimming bubbles and murderous whirlpools all around. These two small rivers usually laid waterless and dead like two dead snakes throughout the whole year. But because of a trench in Paika bridge, there was flood in these two rivers. The flood was so fierce that it can even divide a snake that comes its way into two parts. The submerged villages looked like distant isles. There lied the submerged Nachhipur village: Only the hairy top of the bamboo forest was visible, and also was visible the top of the mango orchard.

Yes! Once the Mangarajpur dam broke like this. Old Govinda Babu scrambled through the old memories. They went floating on a roof and were finally stuck on a little isle. He was twelve or thirteen by that time. He is well acquainted with flood. Today's younger generation do not have much idea about flood. They say there has been some dam at the top that there will be no flood any more. All water shall be preserved in the reservoir. But has man ever conquered water, wind and fire? Oh! The ripened corns were submerged in the flood water. The mountain-like cornstalk floated away in the flood. How could one stop it. It was all God's wish...

Phagu Rout was a school teacher. While leaving home to this small isle due to flood, he managed to bring with him this transistor radio. They were announcing news on flood every half-an-hour. One could wonder they could exhibit more promptness in constructing dams rather than announcing flood news.

Govinda Pattanaik looked in another direction. "What shall I get from listening to that flood announcement? Will that paddy come back? Will that corn-stack come back?" He thought. Hari Dash rushed to listen to the flood-announcement: "The water level of the river is rising because of the release of eleven lakh cusec water from the reservoir. . .The transistor made a bizarre sound and stopped. "Hey! Why did you stop the transistor at the right time?" Hari Dash asked in an irritated voice. His nerves had gotten excited. "When did I stop it? It's getting stopped at times due to power failure." Phagu Rout said. O God! Said Hari Dash.

"The water level shall rise then." The fear in Hari Dash's eyes was visible. Phagu Rout increased his fear by saying: "I think the water level shall rise even more. See the water bubbles are rising." Govinda Pattanaik said: "Listen! It seems as if there is a cloudburst at the river's upper portion. The thunderous roaring of the cloud is audible from a distance. A dark cloud is hanging from the sky." Hari Dash had heard from his childhood days that if there is cloudburst at the river's upper side, then there will be flood ...

In a fearful gesture, Hari Dash looked at the flood water on all sides. He thought why did he come to this Talabani isle while his village folks went onto the canal bridge with their children and livestock. The canal bridge was relatively safer. But he feared that the rising flood water might even submerge the canal bridge. He feared if there was a fissure in the canal bridge. There was no guarantee. Now the Talabani isle might also be submerged under water for the water level was constantly rising. But people say that even the most severe flood has not been able to submerge the Talabani isle. But it's all hearsay. Initially, there was a small palm forest on the isle. But the farmers slowly started cutting the palm trees and there is not even a trace of the forest now. Now the isle lies completely bare. There lies only a 'neem' tree at the top. Hari Dash stared climbing the tree in the fear of the rising water level as he thought that the tree would be a safer place due to its height. But he fell down.

Dasa Pradhan was sitting a little distance away. He shouted: "Hey moron! Why are you climbing the tree? There are three cobras lying circled on the branches. I have seen them."

"O! Snake! Snake!" It looked as if Hari Dash's pair of eyes were bulging out.

Jayee Mohanty is suffering from osteoporosis in his waist. He cannot stand straight. One would wonder how could he climb this isle with such a health condition guiding his way through the flowing streams. It was strange. The irrepressible jest for life had filled his body with a new energy and power.

Hari Dash asked in an apprehensive voice: "If the snakes come down from the tree and bite us?"

Dasa Pradhan kept looking at the flood water constantly and said: "In this flood, the enemies and friends are all alike. There were a black cobra and a boa taking shelter on the same roof on which we also had taken shelter and on which we came floating here." Hari Dash still could not be convinced. He said: "If the rising water submerges this isle and if the snakes come down?"

Jayee Mohanty answered in a taunting voice: "Hey Hari Dash! You are a lone person. If you die, there is nobody behind you to even shed a single drop of tear. Why are you so greedy to live?" There was a tone sarcasm in his voice. Hari Dash played harmonium in the village theatre group. He was the music teacher in that group. He was so indulged in that group, that he did not have time for marriage and thus, remained single.

Hari Dash kept troubling everybody with his unfounded fear. But Jayee Mohanty's taunt got seriously into his mind. Who was after him, truly? He was almost forty. He could not get married till now. His age was also going. If he was swept away in the flood, the village folks won't even search for his body. Then why should he fear so much for his life? But the desire for living is irrepressible. Man likes to live in the midst of all hazards and adversities.

Hari Dash went to a safe distance from the tree and tried to measure the water level. The radio announcement was right; the water level shall rise. By this time, the water level had already risen by a few inches more.

Dasa Pradhan said: "today is the thirteenth day."

Hari Dash asked in a perturbed voice: "So what?"

"The full moon night is right in front. The water-logging does not get cleared therefore. The rising tide is not allowing the river water to enter into the sea. That means the flood water shall rise even further." Explained Dasa Pradhan!

A helicopter was found flying very low and circling in the air. Hari Dash lifted his hands into the air and shouted: "Hey! Save us."

Phagu Rout said: "Hey! Hey! Have you gone mad? Shall the helicopter save us?"

Hari Dash said: "Then why it is flying in the air?"

Phagu Rout answered: "The ministers are greeting you from above. This is a testimony to their service to the people. The newspaper and the radio will be full of praise for these ministers."

Dasa Pradhan was listening to all these while chewing a piece of grass. He responded: "Previously, these ministers were coming on the banana-trunk-made boats risking their lives."

Phagu answered: "You don't understand. Today is the scientific age. Now the flood relief program is carried out in a scientific manner; even the flood is man-made, scientific. The time you are speaking of was a different time when there was flood when Lord Indra poured the Earth with heavy rainfall. Now the engineers make floods by opening the gates of the huge water-reservoirs."

Now two more helicopters came flying in the sky like two giant vultures.

Hari Dash again lifted his two hands into the air and shouted: "Hey Helicopters! Save us. Save us."

The food-packets thrown from the helicopters were falling on the water surface. Hari Dash asked: "What are these packets falling from the helicopters?"

Phagu Pradhan answered: "These are food packets. Have you not heard of food packets being distributed from helicopters during flood time?"

Dasa Pradhan said: "They are distributing the food packets to the fishes. Will they ever reach the people caught up in the water-logging?"

Now they realized they have not eaten anything from yesterday. Their stomachs were burning in hunger. The scorching sun was right over their head. Three or four paper-wrapped food packets fell a few meters away from the Talabani isle. One of them fell at Govinda Pattanaik's reah.

Somebody said: "Hey Pattanaik! Lift those packets. Otherwise, they will be swept away in the stream. Pattanaik stretched his hand to catch hold of the packets. But he drew his hands back and let the food packets drift away. They went floating away in the water."

Dasa Pradhan asked in a stupefied voice: "What happened?" Then he said to himself that it would have been better if he caught hold of those packets. They had not eaten anything for three days. There was not a single morsel of food in their stomach.

Govind Pattanaik told: "I shall not eat this food thrown at us as if we were beggars. In the last flood also, we had not eaten food for three consecutive days. After three days, a few people came on a banana-trunk-made boat and offered us parched rice and jaggery."

"Then was not begged food?" Asked Phagu Pradhan in a taunting voice.

Govind Pattanaik answered: "No! No! They came had

offered us food graciously. There was a sense of respect and dignity in that. It was not throwing food from the sky and taking undue credit." Phagu Pradhan stopped arguing and kept quiet for he knew that there was no point arguing with these old generation people. They had their own stupid and bizarre way of understanding things and they could not be convinced about the new ideas and new ways of living. They were not ready to accept that their generation is gone.

Jayee Mohanty was shouting at somebody: "Hey! You will drown. You will be swept with the current." Nata Kandi had entered deep into chest-height water to get a few food packets floating on the water surface. Holding three/four food packets in his hand, he came out of water.

Phagu Rout shouted: "Give one to me! Give one to me! Nata threw one packet at him.

Jati Nanda was the village priest. His mouth started watering looking at the food packets. But how could he take food from a barber? His sacred thread will be polluted. It will be an act of sacrilege. He has to undergo the purification rites. Still he could not control his curiosity and said in a seemingly indifferent voice: "What are is there inside, boy?

Nata Kandi opened one packet. There were two pieces of bread, some jaggery, two boiled potatoes, one candle light and a few match sticks in a match box. Nata Kandi said to himself: "I wish they kept a few 'bidi's there."

Jati Nanda kept stealthily looking at the open packet. His stomach was burning in hunger. He saw Nata engulfing the breads and jaggery in go and looking at that, as if a sudden fire started burning inside his belly. Then suddenly an old saying came to his mind and it rescued him from his moral dilemma of not taking food form a barber. The saying was: "In utter need, there is no law." It had been said in ancient scriptures that everybody is the same when it comes to the question of hunger. Then Jati Nanda said: "Hey Nata! Has the govt. thrown the packet only for you?" Jayee Mohanty is and old and ailing man. Why don't you give a packet to him?"

Nata was busy engulfing one boiled potato while peeling its skin. He answered in an irritated voice: "When did I say no?" And then he started moving towards Jayee Mohanty to give him one packet."

Jayee Mohanty said: "Hey! Hey! Did you not understand Nata? Give that packet to Jayee Nana[56]."

Jayee Nanda almost snatched that packet from Nata's hand and said in loud voice such that everybody could listen: "In utter need, there is no law." Then he tore one packet and ate up one piece of bread. While chewing, he said: "Hey! Eating this bread is like chewing leather." Saying this, he bit his tongue. How could he say that being a devout Brahmin? Chewing leather . . .?

Phagu Rout got up from his place and ran towards the west side of the isle that had gotten into water like a peninsula.

Nata asked him: "Hey Phagu Babu! Why did you run there so frantically as if caught by a ghost?" Hari also came rushing fearing a new danger.

Nata Kandi shouted: "Mother Ganga! Mother Ganga!" Then everybody looked there. Dasa Pradhana also looked there. Once looking there, he sat down. Govind Pattanaik did not get up from his seat at all. Govind Pattanaik said: "One destitute lady comes floating on a roof." In fact, they

56   A Brahmin priest is called 'Nana' in colloquial language.

had also come floating like that once in another flood. And then he said: "These will exaggerate things like anything."

Nata Kandi started shouting: "Glory to Mother Ganga! Glory to Mother Ganga."

Nobody knew from which village the roof came floating? One pumpkin creeper was still stuck on the roof. A flower had bloomed in that creeper. The lady sat on the roof opening up his hair. Her eyes were wide open. Her eye balls were still an unmoved. They could be seen from a distance. A vermilion mark still sparkled on her head like a piece of dazzling coin. The roof came nearer. Her face was burning bright with slanted sunrays fallen on it.

Nata Kandi shouted again: "Glory to Mother Ganga! Glory to Mother Ganga."

Dasa Pradhan said: "Hey! The destitute lady is floating away. Drag that roof to the shore. If the roof falls in the whirlwind, she will drown and die."

The roof was drifting towards the whirlwind. On it was the destitute lady. She did not utter a single word. If she was not Mother Ganga, would she not have shouted: 'Save me! Save me."

Nobody dared to get into the drifting water. Somebody said: "Don't you all see there is not even a single blink in her eyes?" Jati Nanda said: "Don't you all know the eyes of gods and goddesses never blink?"

Dasa Pradhan shouted: "Hey men! Get into the water. Get into the water and save the lady. She is floating away. I think her family has been swept away by the flood. She is perhaps the lone survivor. She has become deaf and dumb out of fear. It happens like this."

By that time Hari Dash had entered into chest-deep water and was dragging that roof ashore.

"Get down that roof to safety, mother! Where is your village?" Dasa Pradhan asked in a softened voice.

The destitute lady neither got down from the roof nor answered to their questions. She just kept staring dumbfounded at the gathering on the isle.

Dasa Pradhan held the lady's hand softly in his hand and dragged her onto the shore. The moment the lady got into the isle, she burst into tears—unstoppable tears . . . There was no stopping to that wailing.

Dasa Pradhan said: "Leave her in her state. This unfortunate lady has lost everybody of her family. Let her cry. Then only she will come back to her sense. Leave her alone."

The lady kept on crying and fell on the ground. She was senseless. Hari Dash inserted his finger into her mouth and said: "Her teeth have been locked." And then he said worriedly: "What will happen now?"

Dasa Pradhana usually did not get irritated by anything. But Hari Dash had been constantly irritating everybody with his stupid questions. The former's patience came to end and he said in an irritated voice: "What else will happen. You are a bachelor. She has nobody with her now. So, now you will get married to her and then, both will live together. What else . . .?"

Everybody started laughing loudly.

The flood was receding. At places the sand patches were visible like the hard backs of the tortoises. The ripened corns were all swept away. The bamboo jungle of Nachhipur village was also visible. And all those dilapidated earthen houses . . . There was no trace of the Harizan[57] slum. There were no more food packets falling from the helicopters. The flood went away. There were the voices of so many ministers heard on Phagu Rout's transistor.

Nata Kandi said: "Let's all go back to our village. The flood water has almost receded. While going to our Nachhipur village from this Talabani isle, we might encounter knee-deep or at best, waist-deep water at places. Why should we stay here anymore in hungry stomachs? The relief center might have already opened in the village.

Nata Kandi was the first who started walking. Jati nanda followed him. Dasa Pradhana and Govinda Pattanaik also started walking while muttering: "To spend time here on this isle in hungry stomach was perhaps in our destiny." Phagu Rout said: "Hey Jayee uncle! Get up. I will hold you by your arm to help you walk without falling. Keep walking with me." Jayee Mohanty tried to get up from the ground with his bamboo stick. Then he asked: "Where is Hari Dash?"

Hari Dash kept watching the destitute lady under the roof. When will she get back to her senses? The moment she got back to her senses, she looked all around with wide, open eyes as if her eye balls would bulge out and then, fainted again while crying inconsolably.

Hari Dash said: "I cannot go leaving this destitute lady alone."

Jayee Mohanty said in a taunting voice: "This Dash might have stayed all alone throughout his life. Mother Ganga has arranged a bride for her."

---

57   People belonging to the backward castes.

While holding Phagu's hand, Jayee Mohanty started walking down the Talabani isle. There was a sarcastic smile on his lips.

Jayee Mohanty's words as if ignited Hari Dash's hidden desire. The lady was lying flat on the ground. One his breasts laid thoroughly uncovered. Hari Dash covered her breast with her own cloth. He had gotten bored staying in Nachhipur village for so long. That too he was never an original inhabitant of that village. At times, a well-wisher kept asking: "Hari Dash! Will you never start a family?" Hari Dash would mutter: "Who will give his daughter to a forty year old like me?" One would wonder was it so that Mother Ganga had arranged this bride for Hari? She had nobody of her family with her. The flood might have swept away all.

The lady suddenly shouted loudly and then sat straight on the ground.

The reddish light of the setting sun laid scattered on her face. Her eyes were still wide, open.

She started asking: "Where am I? Where are they all? My Kuna and Muna?

Hari Dash was a little assured. She was coming to her senses. By tomorrow morning, she would be alright. He said: "Don't worry. I am here with you. You came floating on a roof that stuck to this Talabani isle."

The lady cried loudly again and fell flat on the ground.

It has been many times since then that she has gotten up, sat straight, shouted loudly and has again fainted. The whole night, the moonlight was flooded on her body.

Till now, Hari Dash had some kind of sympathy and

fellow-feeling for the lady. But suddenly, this flooding moonlight on the lady's body ignited his hidden desire that took the form of an extreme keenness with the lady. Hari Dash kept looking at her with unblinking eyes waiting patiently till she came to senses.

Nobody knew the exact time in the night. Two twittering birds were reeling in the night sky above the Talabani isle. In extreme exhaustion, Hari Dash also slept on the ground. He had anticipated that the lady might come to her sense in the morning.

When Hari got up from his sleep, the whole earth was flooded with the morning's greyish light. The moon was waning in the sky. But where was that lady? The cloth-bundle that she held in her hand while coming floating on the roof was lying out there. But where was that lady?

Hari Dash came outside. But the lady was nowhere. He shouted: "Hey! Where are you?" He did not even know her name. There was a comatose silence all around. Like a lunatic, Hari Dash kept running along the Talabani isle, from this side to that side. How could that lady disappear like this? Or was it dream? Or Nata Kandi was right? Was it Mother Ganga who had come in the lady's form?

In the morning light, Hari Dash could spot the lady's footsteps on the mud at a distance...

****

Black Eagle Books

www.blackeaglebooks.org
info@blackeaglebooks.org

Black Eagle Books, an independent publisher, was founded
as a nonprofit organization in April, 2019. It is our
mission to connect and engage the Indian diaspora
and the world at large with the best of works
of world literature published on a collaborative
platform, with special emphasis on foregrounding
Contemporary Classics and New Writing.